BED ROT BABY

BED ROT BABY

WENDY DALRYMPLE

Quill
&
Crow

Bed Rot Baby

written by Wendy Dalrymple

published by Quill & Crow Publishing House

Printed in the United States of America

Cover Design by Fay Lane

Edited by Cassandra Thompson

ISBN: 978-1-967911-02-8

ISBN: 978-1-967911-01-1 (ebook)

Publisher's Website: quillandcrowpublishinghouse.com

To all the unlikable girls

Chapter One

It's a Tuesday night in January, and I'm sitting across from George at Bosco's Steakhouse again. George has ordered the usual for me: filet mignon with fingerling potatoes and parmesan-crusted broccoli. I haven't eaten all day, and my stomach is in knots as I fork a stalk of broccoli drenched in steak juice across my plate. The soggy floret leaves an unnatural red trail against the white porcelain like some kind of bleeding vegetable. It's another expensive dinner that will likely go to waste.

Tonight, I'm stuffed into a black strapless chiffon dress from BCBG that George bought for me on our last date. It has a tiered ruffled skirt and a sweetheart neckline and is about a size too small. The Agent Provocateur lingerie I'm wearing underneath cinches in my waist just enough so I can zip the damn thing, but the push-up bra underwire is digging into my side, poking at the soft, thin flesh over my ribcage. My hair is big and blonde, and my French manicure is still fresh, with baby pink nails and tips white as snow. I feel awful, but I look good, and that's the most important thing.

My date is dressed in his usual navy suit and tie with the top button of his shirt undone. What's left of his salt-and-pepper hair is swept back from his tanned forehead in a slick of sweat that glistens in the low restaurant lighting. George breathes heavily as he eats, thick fingers gripping his fork and knife as he shovels in mouthful after mouthful of gourmet food with gusto. I worry that he may keel over on me during one of our dates.

"How's the painting going?"

George smiles at me from across the table, grinding a hunk of red meat between his molars. He always reminds me of my dad when he asks me about my work, acting as if he cares when really, he's indifferent. Splotchy crimson patches creep up his neck as he chews, and he makes happy grunting noises of approval. I wonder if his wife also hates watching him eat. I wonder if she has someone special that she spends her week-nights with, too. For her sake, I hope so.

"Fine," I say. "I'm almost done with my current project."

"What are you working on?"

I tilt my head and smile, and for a moment, fool myself into thinking he might actually be interested. George works for a big law firm downtown, and as far as I know, doesn't really understand or appreciate the arts. One time, he asked me who my favorite artist was, and I said Georgia O'Keeffe, and he said he had never heard of her. It's nice that he's always kind and supportive of my artistic endeavors, or pretends to be anyway.

"I've been working on studies of body parts," I say. "When I have the inspiration and time."

George wiggles his eyebrows. "What kind of body parts?"

"Hands, feet, eyes," I say. "All in pastel colors."

"Sounds great," he says. "That's real art. Not like that garbage they hang in office waiting rooms. You know the kind, just a bunch of mess."

"Abstract art?"

"Yeah, like that," he says. "I'm glad you make something that has, you know, *substance*."

"I'm glad you think so." I let out a low, girlish laugh. "Anyway, my work is coming along fine, but I'll need some new canvases and paint soon."

"Don't you worry about that. I'll cover it."

He winks at me and rubs his stockinged foot against mine under the table. George is a foot guy, my weeknight regular for the past three months. While his wife busies herself with scrapbooking classes, Zumba classes, or her book clubs, George buys me expensive clothes and meals I don't eat. Tonight he's enjoying a twelve-ounce porterhouse with a lobster tail and a baked potato. He's already on his third scotch.

"Is your food okay?" George motions toward my plate. A challenge. "We can order you something else."

"No! This is fine!" I say. "Just a little too heavy for me at the moment. I'm going to take my food home and eat it later."

"Good idea."

He gives me another warm, fatherly smile and digs back into his dinner. My stomach clenches as he reaches for a roll and slathers it with a healthy pat of butter. I'm starving now, but I can't eat—not the food he ordered, anyway. The steak dinner is a test, a mind fuck to see just how dedicated to him I really am. It's not that George wants me to completely starve, per se, but he prefers to watch me eat sweets instead. He likes to observe as I consume delicate, dainty desserts, and only in small amounts. Restriction. Control. It's all part of George's kink.

"Any dessert this evening?"

A server appears out of nowhere, smiles, and refills our water glasses. He isn't the same server who brought out our food, but I recognize him as a fellow student from one of my freshman classes at USF. Ethan? Evan? I can't remember. He squints, the corner of his mouth screwed up in a confused expression. I gaze up at him with a fixed grin, frozen as the cogs in his brain churn, trying to figure out where he knows me from.

George smiles and glances at me. "Brittany, do you want anything?"

"Yes, I'll have the tiramisu, please." I nod enthusiastically and smile, smile, smile. My stomach gurgles. Bosco's has great tiramisu. "And a to-go box for my dinner. Please."

"You got it." The server takes the dessert menus, his perplexed, pursed lips curved in a shitty smile. "*Brittany.*"

The server walks away, and a swarm of angry wasps buzzes in my guts. I hate being recognized out in public, especially when I'm on a date.

"Everything okay, baby?"

George rubs his feet against mine again. My face is hot, but my toes are cold.

I smile and nod. "Yeah. Everything's perfect."

"Did you know him?"

"Hmmm?"

"That waiter," George said. "Looks like maybe he recognized you."

"No." I take a controlled sip of water. "I think maybe I just have one of those faces, you know?"

"It's a nice face." George rubs his foot against my calf.

"Thanks. You have a nice face, too."

I break my gaze away from George's reddening cheeks and focus on the fancy chandelier hanging over the dining room. I need to get my head back in the game and be present in the moment. A thousand crystal teardrops glitter in the dim lighting, shooting faceted rainbow patches against the wall like dancing fairies. Each table is covered with a starched white tablecloth with real red fabric napkins to match the thick pile red carpet in the entryway. Bosco's isn't the finest dining establishment in Tampa Bay, but it's George's favorite place to eat, and it's the fanciest restaurant I've ever been to. Even though it's boring going to the same place again and again, I know I should be grateful I'm here.

By the time probably-Ethan brings my tiramisu and coffee to the table, I'm so hungry that I'm no longer annoyed by his presence. A headache throbs between my ears as I savor the first bite of tiramisu slowly and sensually, the way George likes. His eyes glitter as I lick the airy mascarpone cream off the spoon until it's clean. George probably wouldn't have been mad if I ate my dinner first, but he likes the idea of me being a bad girl and skipping dinner in favor of dessert. I do things the way he wants, so I don't spoil our dynamic. Men get bored so easily. I have to keep the tension between us taut and precarious, like a droplet of water clinging to a spiderweb, or he'll drift away from me like all the others.

George finishes his steak while I pick at the tiramisu in little bird bites. He makes small talk about his job and about some home improvements his wife wants to do around the house. I nod and smile behind the coffee cup, leaving a dark cranberry lipstick stain on the rim. The coffee is too hot, and it burns my throat on the way down. I imagine the boiling liquid splashing on the hive of wasps inside of me, melting their wings, quieting their droning.

After dinner, George drives us to a park overlooking the water. I let him smell my shoes, and he masturbates with his eyes closed. When he's finished, he gives me three hundred dollars and drives me to the Bay Vista Condominiums, where I park my car during our dates. He doesn't kiss me or maintain eye contact as we say goodbye, and I wonder if this will be the last time I ever see him. I wait behind the bushes in the Bay Vista parking lot until his taillights disappear into the night.

Cool winter air whips through the condominium breeze-way, and the briny scent of the gulf hits my nostrils. I shiver and pull my faux fur jacket closer around me. I like to park at Bay Vista to give my daddies the impression that I'm doing well financially, and also so I can fantasize about living in a fancy beachfront condo. What would it be like to wake up every day staring at the endless blue-green gulf? What would it be like to watch the sun sink into the horizon from my bedroom window every night?

For a moment, I consider taking a walk on the beach to clear my head, but think better of it. It's far too chilly out, and I'm not properly dressed for a winter stroll by the shore. I dig into my Louis Vuitton bag, find my keys, and unlock my car door. A woman walking a little Yorkie throws me a dirty look as I slide behind the driver's seat. Even in the dark and behind her oversized sunglasses, I can tell that she's sneering at me. Is it because of the way I'm dressed? Or the broken driver's side window of my Corolla?

When the woman's back is turned, I flip her off and start the car. I don't have anywhere that I need to be, no one expecting me, nothing to do. Even though my art project is waiting for me at home, I'm not looking forward to facing my roommate just yet. My stomach rumbles again, and my thoughts drift to junk food, art supplies, and designer underwear. The night is young, and I have money to burn.

Chapter Two

The mall is where I usually ask to meet daddies for a first date. The indoor shopping center is my safe space, always busy and full of people, with good lighting and plenty of things to do. Every time I walk through the glass mall entrance doors, I get a rush of nostalgia-driven endorphins. The sights and smells and sounds of a suburban mall wrap me in a hug, and I'm a teenager all over again. Except now, instead of hanging out with friends and scoping out cute guys, I'm getting my kicks in other ways.

Meeting up at the mall is also a good indicator of whether a prospective daddy will be cheap with me or not. If they don't offer to buy me something on the first date, then there isn't a second date. Every now and then, a prospective daddy will get frustrated and pretend not to understand the dynamics of our proposed situation, and that can lead to trouble. When you meet guys online, you have to be safe and follow the rules. Girls who get careless get killed.

The mall is quiet today, though it usually is once the holidays are over. After everyone returns the Christmas presents they didn't want and spends their gift cards, things slow down again. Even though I like it when the mall is decorated for Christmas, it's harder for me to get what I need when it's busy. During the holiday season, there are too many people and too many watching eyes. From November to the end of December, shops have more staff on the floor, and the security guards are on high alert. Extra safeguards go away when sales die down. Slow season at the mall is harvest time for thieves like me.

My first stop is the food court, where a sprawling sea of empty tables and chairs surrounded by fast food stalls awaits me. I'm a fan of Pizza Bella, but Little Wok is the best restaurant and the most affordable of them all. For $8.99, Little Wok will fill up an enormous styrofoam to-go box of bourbon chicken and fried rice, plus you get an egg roll and a fountain soda. I procure my favorite meal and sit in the food court. I eat half of the bourbon chicken, shoveling plastic spoonfuls into my mouth and swallowing the first two bites without even tasting them. I should have gone home and eaten the steak and potatoes from Bosco's instead, but old habits die hard, and I lost my appetite for George and his overpriced meal.

It's hard to feel alone at the mall. I like getting lost in a sea of faces and being one of many without having to engage in conversation if I don't want to. The mall is fairly quiet tonight, and the only other people in the food court are a couple of older, rough-looking unhoused men and a young mother with her little girl. The little girl gazes at me from under a crop of too-long chestnut bangs as her mother reads a newspaper. I wave at the little girl, and she waves back.

When I've had my fill of sugary, salty chicken, I head toward my next destination, Alice's Art House. It's an expensive place to pick up supplies, but it's the only art store in the mall. The clerk—a young man who definitely isn't Alice—eyes me warily as I admire the rainbow wall of oil paints, my fingers caressing the tubes of cerulean blue and cadmium red. I buy a large canvas with the money George gave me, but I pocket some paints and a couple of sable brushes. I would steal the canvas, too, if it weren't so ridiculously huge.

My next destination is Victoria's Secret, where the real work begins. Two bored-looking teenage girls are behind the counter when I slip through the entrance. Their heads are together, both too involved in gossip to notice me as I slither through the displays. The thumping techno club music drowns out my footsteps and the swish of my dress as I float like a ghost toward a display of delicate things.

The lingerie store is empty and not well-lit, and smells of cotton candy and vanilla. I head straight for a table laid out with lacy thongs and silk bikinis with bows in a mix of bright hues and spring collection prints. I run my fingers over a pair of hot pink mesh panties with neon green ruffles, $12.50 each. The teens giggle in their oblivion bubble as I stash panties in the large shopping bag that holds my canvas and art supplies.

"Hi there! Let us know if you need help with anything!"

Anxiety spikes through my veins. The teens beam at me with their obligatory retail worker smiles as I plunge my hand into the art store shopping bag.

"Thanks." I flash them a smile and move on to the bras.

One of the girls purses her lips and glances at her co-worker. I can't hear what she says, but I know the word *security* when I read it on an anxious retail worker's lips. *Shit.* I hate it when underpaid employees are so eager to follow the rules, itching to bust suspicious shoppers like me. Time for plan B.

I place my half-empty container of rice precariously on the edge of the table with the matching bras and walk towards a display of silky robes. The girls emerge from behind the counter, arms pumping as they make a beeline straight for me. Then, like magic, the to-go container reaches its tipping point, yielding to the laws of nature and the weight of the leftovers within. The container hits the floor with a satisfying styrofoam crunch, and fried rice and saucy chicken splash against the pristine black tile. The two teens scramble to clean up the mess, and I slip out of the store as silently and easily as I entered.

My heart hammers in my neck like crazy as I zip through the mall, triumphant with my spoils. I planned on hitting JCPenney too, but my close call with the Victoria's Secret girls meant it was time to go home. I won't be able to wear this wig to the mall again, but otherwise, my shopping trip proved productive.

The cool night air soothes my burning face as I speed toward the parking lot. My bag of stolen goods swings at my side like a pendulum, making plasticky *thwup thwap thwap* sounds as it slaps against my thigh. I spent less than a hundred dollars at the food court and the art store, but I likely made out with a thousand dollars' worth of underwear and art supplies. I could have taken more, but when you get greedy, you get caught.

The aroma of flame-grilled beef greets me as I open my car door and slip behind the wheel. It was a shame to sacrifice my bourbon chicken, and now I've probably wasted this hunk of meat too. The weather is cold enough, so I consider the possibility that the leftovers might be safe to eat. My adrenaline high is wearing off, and I want to sit in the car and decompress, but I don't want to wait for security to catch up with me either. Time to go home. I turn the ignition and crank my old sedan to life.

My headlights glow, and I scream.

The woman from Bay Vista Condos hovers over the hood of my car, bathed in yellow light. Bloodless lips pout from under a pair of oversized, bug-like sunglasses, her slight frame swallowed by a comically large, black fur coat. Limp blonde hair hangs around her face, grazing supermodel sharp cheekbones and an equally sharp collarbone to match. Did she follow me from the condominium complex? I don't have time to consider why she is lurking in the beams of my headlights before she raises her arms over her head like some kind of symphony conductor.

SLAM.

Her slim white hands land on the hood of my car with surprising force. The woman stares me down through her dark frames, her gaze piercing through the windshield, with that same sneer played out on her lips. The skin on her face is chalky gray, pale enough to show a series of cerulean veins fanning along her jawline just beneath the surface. The entire encounter is freaking me out, but it's her animalistic behavior that shocks me more than the way she looks. Her back arches like an alley cat, like a cobra poised to strike.

"What do you want?"

My voice is shaky. Did I steal her parking spot or something? Is she the wife of one of my daddies, come to enact revenge? My instincts tell me to run, but I can't. I'm frozen, glued to the seat of my car. I'm not a fighter. I'm not prepared for a situation like this. No matter how hard I try to act self-assured and tough, deep down, I am prey. Fuzzy, cute, weak. Stunned and too terrified to defend myself. I convince myself that if I don't move, she can't see me. If I make myself small, she'll go away.

She doesn't go away. The woman darts to the side of my car, and before I can react, a flash of light blinds me.

SNAP.

POP.

WHIZZ.

I wince, my voice whiny and pathetic. "What the fuck is your problem?"

Her hand shoots through my open driver's side window, nails curled like talons. I flail against the woman, screaming and smacking, trapped in place by my seatbelt and by fear. The palm of her hand smacks against the side of my head, and her nails rake against my wig, hooked fingers grasping the locks. She chokes a garbled curse, her claws full of synthetic blonde hair.

In her moment of confusion, the woman recoils, taking my hairpiece with her. My legs finally decide to move as I shift the car into drive and jam my foot on the gas pedal, threadbare tires squealing against the pavement. My self-preservation instincts finally kick in as I peel out of the mall parking lot and leave the woman and my favorite wig in the rearview.

Chapter Three

When I get home, the staircase to my apartment is an obstacle I'm too exhausted to tackle. I live in an apartment complex of inexpensive filing cabinets, two-story buildings that used to serve as student housing for the nearby community college. There's no elevator, so I have no option but to climb the rickety metal exterior stairs that lead to my back door. I clutch the bag of stolen goods to my side, trembling as I begin my ascent.

Climbing the stairs isn't usually this difficult for me, but tonight it feels like an impossible task. I'm reminded of the time Leo pressured me into hiking a section of the Appalachian Trail that I wasn't prepared for. The incline was steep, and I wasn't properly dressed for the impromptu trek. All through the hike, I was terrified of bears and strangers hiding in the woods. Even though he assured me we weren't in danger, I never felt safe. I could still feel eyes watching me beyond the treeline, quiet and calculating, creatures waiting for the opportunity to pounce. A similar feeling of being preyed upon wrapped around my throat now.

My adrenaline reserves are depleted, and I'm crashing hard, but I can't stop moving until I'm safely inside the apartment. All the way home from the mall, I kept my gaze glued to the rearview mirror in case the woman tailed me. Even though it seems like no one followed me home, I couldn't be too careful. She tailed me to the mall, so it wasn't out of the realm of possibility that she would follow me home, too.

I'm probably in shock. That's probably why my body isn't cooperating with me. My head still hasn't entirely wrapped around what happened at the mall. I know I should call my mom for help. I could drive the forty-five minutes to her house and stay the night there just in case the woman followed me, but I don't want to bring my shit to her front door. My mother has been through enough. Besides, I would have to explain my dress and why I was showing up so late at night out of the blue. I could go to a hotel, but I don't have the money to spend either. I've lasted this long being too poor and too proud. What's another day?

My roommate Elaine is already in bed when I enter through our back door. The kitchen smells of the spicy curry she probably made herself for dinner that night. I deposit my leftovers in our fridge, moving as silently as possible so I don't wake her. I'm glad Elaine isn't sitting in the living room, crocheting and watching television, waiting for the opportunity to ream me out. I'm in no mood to talk to her about the rent. Not tonight.

My hands are still shaking as I place my shopping bag on the bedroom floor. My fingers struggle against the zipper, refusing to clamp down on the tiny zip pull. My fingertips finally make purchase and I pull, but the zipper is stuck. All I want to do is peel out of my dress, but it clings to me, pulling in tighter and tighter like a corset with every movement. Anxiety floods my chest, and the bodice constricts and compresses my rib cage. I'm suffocating. Seams pop as I pull at the stubborn fabric, the dress squeezing me like a woven toy finger trap or the coils of a predatory snake.

The popping of plastic zipper teeth signals that I'm free. I'm bathed in relief as the dress finally gives in, the teeth breaking and zipper opening up along my spine like a smile. I drop the ruined dress to the floor, unhook my push-up bra, and toss them both in the hamper. I wince and run my fingers along the tender flesh of my rib cage. Deep red grooves mark the skin from my sternum all the way under my armpits. Fucking underwire.

These clothes that I wear for my clients are cute, but they aren't really me. Jeans and T-shirts are more my speed, but that's not what my daddies want to see. Daddies want me to portray the typical fantasy male gaze aesthetic, where everything about their arm candy is artificial. I've known since puberty that my looks are a superpower; a weapon I can wield. The upkeep for that kind of look is expensive, though, and designer clothes, fake hair, fake nails, eyelashes, and skin treatments cost more than what I could afford on a student budget. Part of me is addicted to the attention, to the process of transformation, and the power I know I hold over others simply by existing. There's a dark side to that attention, though, and the other part of me knows it. The other part of me is sick of pretending to be someone else, sick of continuing to make myself uncomfortable for the sake of aesthetics and pleasing others. Just once, I want to wake up and not give a fuck about what I look like for a day.

My favorite Juicy Couture sweatpants and hoodie set is draped on the back of my vanity chair, and I can't wait to cocoon myself in it. The baby pink velour lounge set was a Christmas gift from my occasional weekend daddy, Ted. He isn't as nice as George, but Ted is generous with gifts and cash. He's into humiliation, and every time he books a weekend with me, I dread our dates and the debasing acts he'll ask me to do. He never crosses a line, but I'm always nervous that he will. Maybe I should stop seeing him.

Now was not the time to think about Ted. After the night I had, all I want is to slip into something comfortable, turn on the television, and rot. I pull on the sweatpants and my old Fiorucci angels t-shirt, then top off the lounge look with the matching hoodie. The soft, plush fabric feels like pure luxury against my skin, like wearing a stuffed animal suit or a cozy blanket. I run my fingertips along the ridge of my velour covered ass and caress rhinestone studs that spell out the word JUICY.

The unfinished self-portrait I hoped to work on that night stares at me from the corner of my bedroom. The composition is turning out pretty well, but I keep making excuses not to finish it. I'm not a very good artist, but I still like the pronounced way I painted my collarbone, outlined in shades of blue, turquoise, and gray. I can't get the shape of my mouth quite right, and my eyes look weird. The altercation with the woman in the parking lot has drained me of any lingering artistic ambition or inspiration I might have had. I flop in bed and turn on the TV. Painting can wait until tomorrow.

The Real World is on MTV, and I let it play without really watching it. My brain is still buzzing, the receptors of my nerve endings aflame as I try to push the frightening events of the evening from my mind. The TV isn't enough of a distraction as I recall the attack over and over again. What did that woman want from me? Her gaunt features dance before my vision as I play out the scenario over and over again. I can't get her out of my head. Nothing was normal about my attacker, from her manner of dressing to the bizarre way her features pinched like some sort of desiccated bug. She looked like Mary Kate Olsen on heroin, like a retired fashion model or a sick socialite with only weeks left to live.

Any normal person would call the police and report the attack, but that was out of the question for me. Not only did I have a closet full of shoplifted goods, but I didn't want to draw the attention of law enforcement if I didn't absolutely need it. As a former daddy once told me, police and other authority figures look on sugar babies like myself as no more than high class hookers who don't deserve protection. I didn't feel very protected before I started seeing daddies anyway.

I dig my Razr phone from the bottom of my purse as the end of the TV episode nears. I know it isn't likely, but I always hold out hope that Leo will text me late at night. I flip the pink phone open, and the interface glows to life. Nothing. I'm too tired and lacking in half-hearted hope to open my laptop and see if he has emailed me. My inbox is likely full of unanswered emails from clients and notifications from chats and message boards. I can ignore them for another night. I fall asleep to the flickering television with my flip phone pressed against my heart.

————

Elaine had already left for work when I emerge from my bedroom the next morning. A small blessing. Even though I never drink, my brain squeezes in my skull as if I have a wicked hangover. I shuffle to the kitchen, pop two aspirin, and down an entire glass of water as my leftovers heat in the microwave. My gaze snags on a note under the fruit bowl on our kitchen table as I wait for my breakfast to warm up. I roll my eyes to the ceiling and open the note, anxious but antici-pating what it would say.

Rent is three days late. Please leave your half on the kitchen table by the end of the day, or we need to have a talk. I can't afford to keep floating you.

- E

Elaine is a pharmacy manager, and I know she makes loads of cash. She's also super frugal because she's trying to save money for a down payment on a home. I know for a fact that she could easily float my half of the rent until I can pay her back, but she just doesn't want to. I snort and crumple the note into a ball. I know I'm being a shit, but part of me resents her. Everything is so easy for Elaine; she came from a good family. She had a scholarship and finished school at the top of her class. She's bringing in the big bucks while I scrape by.

Jesus, I sound pathetic. It's not Elaine's fault that she gets a good hand in life and I get all of the shitty cards. I've been in this self-pity shame spiral for so long that it's hard not to think any other way. I'm going to try to do better for Elaine. For myself. Unfortunately, having a better attitude won't magically help me pay the rent, so I need to get to work. Thankfully, I was able to replenish my stock at the mall last night.

The microwave dings, and I bring the reheated leftovers to my bedroom to begin work for the day. My eBay notifications have piled up since the last time I logged on. Of the dozen Victoria's Secret listings I ran, ten were finished, all with bids of $60, $80, and even $100. All of my buyers were men I had met in chat rooms. Selling my intimate goods through eBay was a safer, more secure method than selling direct, and getting paid has never been a problem. None of my customers ever try to get a refund for women's underwear. I can imagine it would be an embarrassing thing for a man to explain to the bank or their wives.

With my listing sales confirmed, I spritz the lace undies with BCBGirls Max Azria Sexy perfume, snip off the price tags, and pack them in mailers one by one. The men who bid on my listings all think they are buying underwear from my personal collection; thongs, briefs, and bras that have been in contact with my skin. The underwear I usually wear is sensible, boring, and functional without a lick of lace or bows or mesh. I'm in the business of selling fantasy, and my plain Hanes panties simply won't do. Besides, I need my real underwear.

An hour goes by as I finish packing undies and updating my listings. It would be another couple days before my payments cleared from eBay, so Elaine would have to keep her shirt on for now. Still, it's a relief to know that rent money was on the way, and all I have to do is drop the packages off at the post office. Leo never thought I would be able to sell anything on eBay. Well, look at me now.

I pull my dark hair into a messy bun, slip into a pair of sherpa-lined UGGS, and stash my packages in a tote bag from Old Navy. My Juicy velour lounge set is comfy enough for sleep and dressy enough to run errands, two things that are of the utmost importance when I'm off-duty. I hate to be uncomfortable when I don't have to be.

Before I head out the door, I check my phone for any new messages from George or Ted, or maybe even Leo, but there's nothing. I don't expect my mother to text me; she doesn't have a cell phone. But it would be nice to hear her voice, so I pull up her name in my phone book. I listen to the phone ring, and go straight to her answering machine.

"Hi there, this is Susan Miller. I'm not in right now. Please leave your name and a message, and I'll get right back to you."

"Hey, Mom," I say, but my throat closes. Tears betray me and spring to my eyes. I didn't realize how much I needed to hear my mother's voice. I clear my throat and swallow it down. "I just wanted to call and say hey. Um, call me later when you aren't busy. Bye."

Shit. I hate it when I cry. My eyes get all red and puffy, and I look like hot garbage. I can't go out looking like this. I go to the bathroom and splash my face with cold water. I'm suddenly very tired and my body is heavy, as if a weighted blanket were draped around my shoulders. I can't stop crying.

I drop the tote bag of packages, turn on the TV, and flop

back down on the bed. I flip through the daytime TV channels past commercials for air freshener and diapers until I find a soap opera. Some doctor with perfect teeth and a tan is telling a woman wearing makeup in a hospital bed that she only has a few more days left to live. God, it's already the afternoon. I missed my favorite game shows, and now I'm stuck with General Hospital. I sink into my bed, caressing the high-thread-count sheets.

There's no one I want to see. No one who needs me. Nothing that I need to do. It's just me, my bed, and my self-pity. I pull the covers over me and let my vision glaze over as the soap opera credits roll. The post office will have to wait another day.

Chapter Four

Neither dreams nor nightmares fill my sleep, only an endless, blissful blackness that envelops me, folding me into its fluid arms like an oil slick in the ocean. When I wake, it's dark outside, and Elaine has left another note under my door. I somehow managed to sleep the rest of the day away, and yet, I still don't feel refreshed. I also have a missed call from my mother and a new text from George.

> Hey baby, can't meet up tomorrow like usual. Will call you soon. Be good and don't eat any dessert until I see you again.

Ugh. I toss the phone across the bed and try to think of a response. Even though I'm relieved about not having to suffer through another dinner with George, the text is still bad news. If I don't spend time with him, I don't get paid. Sometimes I think I might make more money as a dancer, but I have neither the confidence nor the coordination to go up on stage. Other sugar babies get their daddies to buy them cars and pay their rents and student loans, but I can't even keep a client interested for more than a few weeks. George has been my longest-running daddy so far, and now I get the impression that he's done with me, too. I must be doing something wrong to drive them all away. Then again, I shouldn't be surprised. I don't really care enough to try to improve my sugar baby performance and personality. My heart isn't in it, and it's starting to show.

My sheets stink like dried sweat and stick to my skin as I stretch myself awake. The bones in my hips and shoulders crack as I lengthen my body, and a dull ache settles into my joints. My fingers are stiff and hurt when I flex them, and my thoughts turn to my great-grandmother, Viv. She was in her mid-nineties when I was a little girl. My mother and I would visit her in the nursing home every so often, and I was always horrified by her rheumy fingers, bony knuckles, and paper-thin skin over blue-veined hands that curled into painful fists. The memory of how I reacted to her makes me ashamed now. In the back of my mind, I always wondered if her fate would also be mine someday: twisted, in pain, and alone.

The popcorn ceiling overhead mocks me as I lie in bed with my eyes wide open, bones throbbing and brain on fire. The finish on the ceiling is yellowed with time and looks more like cottage cheese than popcorn to me. The thought of curdled milk and thin, runny whey makes me gag. Bile rises in my throat, and the urge to purge pulls me out of bed. I stumble toward the bathroom on shaky legs and barely reach the toilet as the remnants of my steak dinner hit the bowl. Fuck. I knew I shouldn't have eaten those leftovers.

I rinse my mouth and face and take a hesitant glance in the mirror as I brush my teeth. I expect to look bad, but my shitty reflection still surprises me. My hair is greasy and dull and hangs in clumps at my shoulders, but that's nothing compared to my waxy complexion. My skin is paler than usual, and my undereyes look like I survived a round in the ring with Mike Tyson. Under any other circumstances, I wouldn't be caught dead leaving the house looking this way, but I need to send off my packages if I want my eBay business to remain in good standing.

There's also the issue of rent and keeping my roommate from kicking me out. I write a note and take the money I have leftover from last night and shove it under Elaine's door. I'm still short about five hundred dollars, but I should have the rest of it to her by the end of the week. It's not much, but it should shut her up until my payments come through. I still need money for gas and groceries, so I might scour my wardrobe later and unload a few items at the resale shop. Anxiety builds in my chest as I mentally calculate how much the clothing exchange shop will give me for the last three pairs of designer jeans in my closet. I don't think it will be enough. Every waking moment of my life is devoted to thinking about the next step, the next hustle, the next bare minimum payment. I could make it all go away if I just moved back home, lived with my mother, and got a regular job again. But I know the darkness would eventually creep back in, and I would just slide back into my old habits like I always do.

After a great effort, I make it out the door and drive to the nearby post office. The usually brilliant blue sky is overcast today, and my sensitive eyes are grateful for the shade. Sometimes the Florida sun is so bright that simply staring at the sidewalk can singe your retinas. Blacktop parking lots in the middle of summer make your skin feel like it could drip right from your bones. Living here isn't for the weak; you have to be scrappy, capable of withstanding extreme humidity and heat, and the extreme people who call this place home. I used to be scrappy.

The atmosphere inside the post office is just as dreary as the January sky. Everyone looks as miserable as I feel, weighed down by packages and annoyed at having to wait for service. I stand in line and pray my only remaining credit card has enough balance on it to send my packages. If the card doesn't go through, I'm screwed.

A woman at the head of the line is dressed in a large trench coat with oversized sunglasses to match, and I'm reminded of the woman from the mall parking lot. Part of me hopes that I never see her again. Another part of me wants to track her down and ask what the fuck her problem was. Either way, the memory of her sneering, thin lips and witch-like hands sends a shiver down my spine. I really liked the wig she snatched off my head, too.

My credit card clears, and the post office takes the packages off my hands. My relief is brief as I remember that I still owe Elaine the rest of my rent money, and after that, my cell phone bill, and a minimum payment to the credit card companies. The trip to the post office has left me drained, so haggling with the clothing resale clerks will have to wait. Fortunately, I have another somewhat risky, yet tried-and-true trick up my sleeve for making some quick cash.

Even though my face looks like hot garbage at the moment, my real money makers are still in pretty good shape. When I get home, I slip out of my sandals and examine my freshly manicured toes and the delicate lines of my smooth, shapely feet. It was these fancy feet that landed me a date with George in the first place. No wonder he's losing interest in me; beyond his foot fetish, I have little else to offer him. Fortunately, George isn't the only one who appreciates my well-cared-for feet. With a little lotion and some nail polish touch-up, I'm ready to go.

I got into selling foot pics in high school as a joke, and then quickly learned that it was an easy way to make extra cash. The chat rooms were harder to navigate back then, but as a lonely, untethered teen, I had nothing but time to explore them. I stay out of the chat rooms for the most part these days, usually only dropping in to post about my available eBay offerings. There's always someone who wants to try and get something out of me for free, and that in itself is annoying and exhausting. Sometimes, the dirty talk and requests for additional pictures that go along with selling foot pics to strangers can get to be a little much, so I don't do it all the time. But at the moment, I'm desperate enough to do just about anything, and lying down is all I have energy for. Even answering messages and posting in my usual chat rooms wipes me out, and all the typing makes my wrists throb.

The front door opens and closes, and is followed by the familiar sound of Elaine rummaging through the fridge. It occurs to me that I haven't eaten anything since the rancid leftovers I puked up. Junk food usually makes me feel better in times like this, but I'm not even hungry, and even if I were, there wasn't anything to eat. Moments later, Elaine's bedroom door opens, and there's a knock at my door.

"Hey. Are you in there?" Elaine's muffled voice is loud and angry on the other side of the door. "This isn't enough to cover rent."

"I'm getting paid in a few days," I say. "You'll get the rest then."

"You know, our lease is coming up for renewal in March," Elaine says. "I've decided to move in with Leticia."

Regret wiggles into my chest. Elaine has mentioned that she wanted to move in with her girlfriend before, but this almost sounds like a threat. She's just bluffing. I'm sure she is. I swallow, clear the lump in my throat, and try to sound as unimpressed as possible.

"Gee, thanks for the heads up."

Elaine huffs, her disgust audible through the closed door. "You're not going to be able to live this way much longer, you know. Good luck finding another roommate that will put up with your shit."

"Good luck not being a huge bitch," I grumble just loud enough for her to hear.

Elaine stomps away, and my pulse quickens. March. If she's serious this time, then that leaves me with a little less than two months to either find another roommate to take her place or to move somewhere else. Tears spring to my eyes, and again, I allow myself to cry. I feel like shit for letting Elaine down. This wasn't supposed to be my life. I'm not supposed to be wasting away in an apartment with no money, no boyfriend, and a roommate who hates me.

Fucking Leo. I don't know why I trusted him. I should have known by the way my dad treated my mom that love and romance are just a fantasy. Leo was always so good with words and with his hands that I wanted to believe. I know now that I was a fool, just like I was a fool waiting for his texts and phone calls that would never come. My daddies and the men who buy my photos are all fooling themselves, too. Everyone wants to think they're so special and that someone out there cares about them, but it's all fake. We only love ourselves in the end.

I glance back at my laptop screen and am relieved to see messages, payments, and requests for photos flooding my inbox. Some orders I can fulfill with photos from my archives, depending on how specific the request is, but others I'll need to create brand new. I have images of my feet with toenail polish painted in every color of the rainbow; photos of my toes buried in the sand, photos of my feet splashing in the bath. One time, a client even requested a photo of my feet buried in a gallon of ranch dressing with white sauce squishing between my toes in close-up shots. So long as my clients' requests aren't illegal or in poor taste, I try to fulfill them.

My eyelids flutter, heavy under their own weight, as I email pictures $5, $10, $20 at a time. It hardly seems worth the effort, but it all adds up, and after I pay rent, there's always another payment or bill due. It's a never ending cycle, a fucked up rollercoaster and I don't know how to get off, or if I even deserve to. Maybe this is the way my life is supposed to be. Struggling. Depressed. Always living on a wing and a prayer, making things work by the skin of my teeth. Just once, I'd like to be able to feel like I can breathe.

I wasn't always this pathetic. I used to have my shit together. Money was always an issue, but I always made rent and always paid my own way. The sugar baby life was supposed to bring me more money than I had been making at the grocery store, but so far, I haven't been able to make it work for me. Maybe it's because my heart isn't really in it. Maybe if I were more enthusiastic, my daddies would have bought me a nice car or given me a bigger weekly allowance by now. Like everything else, even in the sugar baby life, I've been selling myself short.

The day gets away from me as I work from my bed, sinking deeper and deeper into the mattress. The heat of my laptop radiates through my pelvis, warm and comforting against my aching bones like a hot water bottle or a hug. My phone pings next to me, but I'm too tired to answer it. I close my eyes and ease further into my mattress, the musty bed sheets enveloping me like a holy, ancient shroud. A vision of the woman with thin lips and sunglasses flashes before my eyes just before I let the inky wave of sleep wash over me again.

Chapter Five

"Hey, baby. Something's come up and I have a free weekend. I was wondering if you were available to join me for a day date and then dinner after. Maybe even for an overnight. Call me back. Bye, baby."

I listen to George's voice message over and over again the following morning, and my dry lips crack into a smile. Thank God. Maybe he wasn't completely bored with me just yet. An entire day with George would be exhausting, but it was exactly what I needed. In twenty-four hours, I could earn enough cash to get Elaine off my back and maybe even get a few new art supplies out of the deal, too. For an overnight, I could charge him enough to clear me for the rest of the month. This was the break I'd been waiting for. I needed to shower and get dressed, but first I had to find the energy to get out of bed.

My legs are made of sand as I rise, the bones in my ankles

crunching and crackling beneath my weight. I make my way to the bathroom and sit on the toilet, but nothing much happens. Did I drink anything yesterday? I can't remember. This stomach bug is kicking my ass, and I need to hydrate and eat something if I'm going to be in good enough shape for a full work weekend. Goodness knows I won't be allowed to eat much in front of George. Better fill up now.

Elaine is sitting in the breakfast nook and reading a self-help book with her sad toast and tea as I plod toward the kitchen. I open the fridge, hopeful that there's something in there to eat that's mine, even though I haven't grocery shopped in ages. There isn't anything, of course, so I go to the sink and pour a glass of water. All the while, I can feel Elaine burning daggers into my back with her eyes, her breath hot and heavy as she seethes behind her book. I scrape the back of our pantry cabinet with my fingertips and discover a single forgotten instant oatmeal packet that belongs to me. Breakfast.

"I've got a big job tomorrow." I tear open the packet and pour the oatmeal into a bowl. "I'll have the rest of the rent to you by Sunday night."

Elaine puts her book down and gives me a dead-eyed stare. "You look like shit. Are you sick or something?"

"What do you care?" I pour water onto the dry cereal and place the bowl in the microwave.

"I care."

I roll my eyes. "Okay."

"I thought we were friends," she says. "You've been shutting me out for months. I'm upset with you, but I'm also worried."

The microwave dings. I pull out the steaming bowl and stir the oatmeal, avoiding her glare. "So."

"So, I know what you're up to," she says.

"And what is it that I'm up to, Elaine?"

"I know you meet men for money," she says. "Look, I'm not one to judge. I don't care what people do, but it seems dangerous. And it doesn't seem to be making you very happy either."

"Who *is* happy?" I snort, still stirring my oatmeal. "Don't worry about me. I'm a big girl. I can take care of myself."

"You know, you don't have to keep doing this. I can get you a real job at the pharmacy."

"I have a real job," I say, blowing on the hot cereal. "I'll get you your money. I'll be out of your hair in a few months, and you won't have to worry about me anymore."

Elaine frowns. "And what about your art?"

"What about it?"

"Are you still working on anything?" She asks. "Leticia can still get you into her gallery downtown whenever you're ready."

"I don't need your girlfriend to host a pity art show for me."

"It wouldn't be out of pity. You're good," Elaine says. "Like, really fucking good. I hate to see you waste your talent."

"I'm a hack. Besides, I'm expressing myself in different ways these days."

"Whatever." Elaine shakes her head and picks up her book.

I breeze past her with my bowl of oatmeal and tepid water

toward my bedroom. There's a noticeably distinct smell as I re-enter the room, which grows more pungent as I near the bed. I must have become nose blind to the scent, but now, it makes my nostrils twitch. The smell is tangy, somewhere between the stench of a locker room and the savory umami of delicious aged cheese. I need to wash my sheets and clean up before Elaine complains about my room, too.

Leticia. Even though I trust her judgment more than the pretentious art kids I tried to hang out with, I know she's just saying my work is good to be nice. We met Leticia through Leo; she was his manager at the gallery where he worked right before we broke up. I like Leticia, and at least Elaine got something good out of the time I spent with him.

The half-finished canvas I've been struggling with for months stares at me as I sit on the edge of the bed and choke down my bland breakfast. The brush strokes on the canvas are flat and uninspired, the subject staring back with an expression that can only be described as indifference. The truth is, I've lost confidence in my ability to create. There's nothing inspired or unique at all about my self-portrait, just like there's nothing inspired or unique about me. I was always too bland and normal for the art kid crowd, and now I'm too boring for the sugar daddy life, too. Elaine doesn't know what she's talking about either. There's absolutely nothing special about my art, or about me. Being a working artist was a stupid dream from when I was a stupid kid. Thinking differently is a waste of time.

I place my half-eaten bowl of oatmeal on the ground and pick up the pastel abstract portrait. Most of the brush strokes are lazy, but I try to find one good, positive thing about the piece. I suppose I still like the color palette I selected, a wash of lifeless gray and pale pink, dusty blue and butter yellow. I regard my own image, realizing that I've made my eyes too small, but then, that's how they look in real life. I grab a palette knife from my supply caddy and slash the center of the canvas.

My pastel oil paint face splits in two.

———

Two hours later, I'm showered, dressed, and slightly more energetic. Elaine is gone and the apartment is quiet again, but now that there's a little bit of money in my account, I'm itching to get out and spend. I need something nice to wear for my weekend with George, and something else to eat besides oatmeal. The mall is calling my name.

My close call at Victoria's Secret makes me wary of being seen at my usual haunt, so I drive an extra fifteen minutes to the mall in the next town over. On the way, I pass Bay Vista Condos and shudder. Which condo does the woman who assaulted me live in? If she even lives there at all, that is. Maybe she's like me, a counterfeit. A trespasser. Either way, the real terror of seeing that awful woman again fills me with anxiety.

I pull into Countryside Mall and park near the movie theater entrance. Before I go in, I check my reflection in the visor mirror to assess myself. My pallid complexion and dry, cracked lips make me look like an ill Victorian child. I reach into my purse to grab some lipstick and realize I missed a call while I was driving. Leo's phone number flashes on the screen, and my heart stops. He left a message. I almost drop my phone as I scramble to listen to the voicemail.

"Hey, uh, it's me."

Leo clears his throat. Electronic nursery rhyme music is playing somewhere in the background.

"Elaine called me and asked if I would check up on you. Violet is keeping me pretty busy these days, but if you ever need to talk, you can call me. I, um… I hope you're still seeing that counselor. I know it helped me when I was going through a hard time. Anyway, please take care of yourself. I'll, uh, be in town soon. Maybe we can meet up and talk. Okay. Bye."

I listen to the voicemail again and again, training my ear to see if I can pick up the coo of a baby crying, or the light footsteps of Leo's dance teacher fiancée. Fucking Elaine. Fucking Leo. I must be all cried out because normally, a call like this would send me into a complete tailspin. But this time, I don't feel anything. I want that numb sensation to linger, want to make sure I don't feel anything again for a long fucking while. The mall is the perfect place to get my fix.

I check the marquee to see what movies are playing and what's showing next. Options are slim, and *Underworld: Evolution* is the only thing that looks halfway decent. I buy myself a matinee ticket and head straight for the concession stand. The woman behind the counter looks to be of retirement age and has no patience for me as I select a tray of nachos, a large Diet Coke, chocolate-covered raisins, and a pack of sour gummy candies. The concession woman rings my snacks up with a judgey, stank-face expression. I want to tell her to fix her fucking face, but I also don't want to get kicked out of the movies before it even starts. Instead, I give her my most terrifying smile, take my treats, and find my seat in the darkened auditorium. I'm the only one in the theater.

Time passes in a blur as I watch Kate Beckinsale, bathed in blue light, shooting up poorly made computer graphic werewolves. My hand hits the bottom of the nacho tray, and I bring the plastic container to my mouth, my tongue searching the curved grooves to lick clean every last bit of chemical-laden liquid cheese. Halfway through the movie, I get up to refill my soda and buy a large popcorn. Thankfully, the woman behind the counter had left and was replaced by an indifferent teenager. By the time the movie is over, my snacks are gone, and I don't even remember what I watched.

The movie theatre gorge cost quite a bit of my foot photo earnings, but it was worth it for a few hours of mind-numbing solace. I float on a binge high through the mall toward my next score, shoving calorie counts and dollar amounts far from my thoughts. I can't get my money back, and I don't want to purge what I ate, even though the rush of vomiting would give me another easy high. I'll have to get my dopamine hit from taking unnecessary risks instead.

Dillard's is always easy to steal from, and they usually have a good selection of the brands I like. Most items under a certain price point don't even have anti-theft tags, and the store is always understaffed, especially during the slow season. This particular Dillard's is also huge and tomb-like during the early weekday hours: 100,000 square feet of carpeted, air-conditioned liminal space. Sometimes shoplifting is so easy, it almost isn't even a thrill.

I need new things for the weekend, so thrill or no, I still have to shop. Even though George is a foot guy, for whatever reason, he doesn't seem to care that much about which style of shoes I wear. He prefers it when I wear ruffles and satin—skimpy, girly things that show off my figure and make me look innocent but naughty. I would kill for a new Betsey Johnson dress, but the only store that carries them in the area was in Tampa, and the boutique is impossible to shoplift from. Maybe I'll try to talk George into taking me shopping there over the weekend to pick up a few new things.

After quickly scanning the racks, I settle on a floral turquoise wrap dress from Nanette Lepore's spring line. I'm about to stuff a satin and lace camisole from Le Mystere in my coat pocket when I notice a sales clerk heading my way. Adrenaline numbs my limbs, and I sprint for the exit. I sail through the electronic scanners at the entrance to the store and leave the sales clerk in my dust.

Back out in the mall, the promenade is filled with teenagers and young mothers pushing strollers. I forgot that it was Friday, and now the stores and walkway are a little too busy for my tastes. I still need to hit Nordstrom Rack for a few more items in case George makes our date a full weekend affair, but as I bump into rowdy teens and exhausted women with babies, the anesthetic of my shoplifting high begins to wear off. Even though I'm dressed comfortably in my favorite Juicy tracksuit, I still feel like my chest is constricted, like I can't breathe. I pass Nordstrom Rack and head straight for the bathroom instead, where I retch up my concession stand meal.

A middle-aged woman in a housecoat with sculpted 1970s hair gives me a judgmental side-eye as I approach the shared sink. I smile at her with popcorn vomit-crusted teeth. She makes a sound of disgust and moves away from me as I rinse my mouth. I feel a little better, but only marginally.

I avoid looking in the mirror this time.

Chapter Six

My head hurts as I slap the flip top of my phone closed and stare at my laptop screen. There are new orders for underwear and foot pictures, including one where I bury my toes into a pile of Beanie Babies for some reason. I don't know where I'll find a bunch of Beanie Babies, but I'll send him a quote for $150 and see if he bites. I don't have time to fulfill the custom orders before my weekend with George, so they'll have to wait until I return.

It's Friday evening now, and George hasn't called back to

confirm our plans for the weekend. I'm getting nervous because even though he hasn't ever flaked out on me, I've seen this pattern with other clients and daddies before. Men love the fantasy of our arrangement, the idea of keeping me in their back pocket and at their beck and call. But after a while, it isn't worth the effort for them anymore. That, or they want something new. I get it. For them, the effect of being a daddy and keeping a sugar baby is like shoplifting for me. Even though I understand what our relationship really means, the rejection still hurts. I'm not useful to them anymore, and the reality stings.

Still, if George does make good on his word, I need to be ready to go. My bags are packed with my new Nanette Lepore dress and a few other items in my closet that I know he likes. I wish I had time and money to get a new blonde wig like the one the woman in the parking lot stole. I'm going to have to tell George I moved and find a new swanky condo to park in if he wants to continue seeing me. I can't risk running into that woman again. My heart won't be able to take it.

I flip my phone open again, and my finger hovers over Leo's number in my phone book. On one hand, I want to talk to him and assure him that I'm doing just fine, great in fact. Let him know that I'm better off without him. Let him know that his hipster Brooklyn life with his baby and fiancée is the furthest thing that I could ever want. That I'm *so* happy for them, really and truly. Another part of me wants to tell him to fuck off and delete his number. I know that I never will, though. I guess I like to keep Leo in my back pocket, too. Well, not anymore.

I delete Leo's number and all of his texts, and call my mother instead. After a few rings, she picks up.

"Hi, baby!" My mother's voice is singsongy and high. It's Friday night, and she's likely halfway through a bottle of Sutter Home Moscato.

"Hi, Mom," I say. "What's new?"

"Oh, you know, not much. I had to take Gladys to the vet this week. She has a cyst that needs to be drained."

"I'm so sorry." Gladys is one of my mother's three Persian rescue cats.

"What's new with you, baby?" she asks, her voice soft. "Been working on anything?"

I glance at the corner of my room. My destroyed self-portrait lies in a heap on a pile of dirty laundry. The canvas I bought at the mall is still in the bag in my closet with the stolen brushes and paints.

"Not really," I say. "Actually, I haven't been feeling too well."

"Did you get your flu shot?" she asks. "I know Elaine can get you one. You shouldn't skip it."

"No. I forgot. I'll get to it."

"Good, good. Say, maybe you can come over this weekend and we can have dinner? Or I'll come out your way and we can see a movie. I hear that Lord of the Ring movie is pretty good."

"It's Lord of the Rings, not Ring," I say. "Anyway, I don't think I can. I'm supposed to work all weekend. The gallery is having a big event, and it's all hands on deck."

"Oh, well, you rest up then," she says. A muffled purr vibrates my ear, and my mother laughs. "Penelope, get down!

Speaking of the gallery… You haven't been talking to Leo again, have you?"

My heart jumps at his name. "No. Of course not. I deleted his number."

"Because I know how hard it must be for you. You can talk to me about it any time. When your father up and left…"

"Mom, it's okay, really. I'm over it," I lie. "Listen, I'll come over next weekend—maybe I'll even stay the night. We can make dinner and watch movies."

"That would be nice," she says. "I love you, baby."

"I love you, too," I say, picking at my pinky nail. "Give Gladys, Penelope, and Margaret a scratch for me."

"I will. G'night."

"Night."

It sucks that I have to lie to my mother about what I do for a living, but there's no other way around it. I never even worked at the gallery either, I just told her that so she wouldn't get worried after I got fired from the grocery store. What she doesn't know won't hurt her, or something like that.

I flip the phone closed, toss it on the bed, and take stock of my surroundings. My room is atrocious, and I should clean it before I leave for the weekend, but the prospect of going to the laundromat is too much. I grab some large garbage bags from the kitchen and begin bagging everything up instead. I strip the sheets from my bed, horrified at their rank condition. There's a greasy, crusty outline on the fitted sheet where I lay that makes me gag just looking at it. Maybe I need to change my birth control, or maybe something else is making my hormones all out of whack. As if I could afford to go to a doctor. If it weren't for the free clinic, I wouldn't be on birth control at all.

I lay my only spare flat sheet on the bed and finish tidying up my room. Even after vacuuming, taking out the trash, and wiping down my vanity and side table, the space still feels stagnant and grimy. Cleaning leaves me winded and dizzy, and I have to stop and take breaks for even the simplest tasks. It's too cold out to open the window, but I do it anyway to let some fresh air in. Lifting the window is a Herculean task. Even though I don't normally have much strength in my arms, being unable even to open a window makes me feel ancient.

A clanging sound catches my attention as I stare down into the alleyway behind our apartment. The street lamp shines on our garbage receptacle like a spotlight, an eyesore that won't be hidden even in the dark. I half expect to see a family of opossums or raccoons hanging out amongst our discarded banana peels and toilet paper rolls. Instead, a pair of wide, round eyes shines back up at me through the dead of night.

Except, they aren't eyes. They're lenses. Dark sunglasses. A wisp of hair. Sneering lips spread out over pearly little teeth. It isn't a small mammal or rodent. It's the woman from the condo, from the mall parking lot, and she's staring up at me from her crouching position in the dark. She's found me.

"I see you!" I shout. "Get the fuck away from my house!"

The woman hisses and backs into the shadows. I was scared of her before, but now, I'm pissed. Who the fuck does she think she is, following me, watching me, tormenting me like this? A much-needed burst of energy floods my limbs, and I tear out of my apartment down the stairs toward the dark alley.

I catch the flick of her coattails as she rounds the corner of my apartment block into another alley. She's fast, but despite being drained of energy, I'm somehow able to keep up. Why is she afraid to face me this time? She already assaulted me. I wasn't going to let her get away with creeping on me, too.

"What the fuck is your problem, lady?" I yell out, turning the corner. Her designer heels echo against the pavement as I give chase, their clacking slower and slower. I've caught up with her again. "Come back here, you little bitch! Come on, let's go!"

She half turns back to look at me as I gain ground. Even in the harsh parking lot lighting, I can tell she looks different. Her hair is fuller and shinier, and her lips and cheeks are plumper, like she got Botox or filler or something.

"Brave enough to attack me, but not brave enough to face me, huh?" A wild, explosive laughter rips from my lips. Who does this bitch think she is, coming into *my* territory? She won't get away with it. Some long-forgotten, feral part of me is breaking through, and I like it. "Come on, lady, let's end this!"

I'm nearly caught up to her now. I could almost reach out and grab her. I lunge, and my fingertips graze the soft fur of her coat.

She turns back and hisses at me again, dodging my outstretched hand with impressive agility. She hunches over, and I blink, and then the next thing I know, she's hovering in mid-air. I stop dead in my tracks, stunned as she floats silently up into the night like some kind of fucked up Mary Poppins. She lands on the roof of an apartment block and hisses at me one last time before scampering off into the night.

I stand in the parking lot in a daze for I don't know how

long. There's no use trying to make sense of what just happened. There was no way to make it work in my mind. Barring some special effects film department setting up an elaborate hoax on my behalf, there's no way that skinny, freakish woman—or *anyone* for that matter—could have scaled the building like that. Let's face it, she *floated* for fuck sake. My brain won't accept what I have just seen.

The altercation was dissolved, the woman was gone, and my burst of energy was drained, taking the last of my motivation with it. It was time to get back to bed. I walk toward my apartment, confused, but empowered with a sense of vengeance. Along the way, I pass the dumpster where the woman had been staked out, hiding and watching me. Stalking me. There on the ground is a mass of flaxen hair. I bend down and pick it up, the synthetic hairs full of leaves and debris. My favorite wig.

Chapter Seven

That night, I dream that I am made of cake.

I am having dinner with George again in some fancy restaurant. He hands me a fork and makes me eat tiny little bites of myself. Leo is our waiter, but he's eighteen again, like when we first met. He looks like he did during our freshman year of college, baby-faced with short hair and no beard. He brings George's dinner to the table on a platter, and it's a steak in the shape of an infant in the fetal position. Before George takes a bite of his baby steak, I tell him I need more money. For some reason, my mom's Persian cats are also there, and George is feeding them little bites of tender meat.

And then I wake up.

Muted yellow light illuminates my bedroom, bathing everything I own in a piss colored hue. My fresh bed sheets are sticky and smelly, and my skin is slick with grease and sweat. There's a text message from George that says he'll pick me up at the Hilton at noon, and to be dressed for a fancy lunch date.

A groan escapes my lips when I realize I only have two hours to get ready. I really don't want to go out. I don't want to have to entertain George or anyone else anymore. All I want to do is lie in bed, watch TV, and rot. But there's work to do and money to earn, so I have to get up.

A fancy lunch date with George probably means dining at some country club. I mentally prepare myself for an afternoon spent watching him slurp oysters and get day drunk on bourbon while he talks to me about his law partners or his dog's skin allergy. If I am lucky, he'll get so drunk that he'll fall asleep in whatever hotel suite he rents before asking me to do anything disgusting.

The skin on my back feels like it's ripping off as I tear myself from the sweat-drenched bed sheets. I hobble to the bathroom on creaky joints, turn on the water, and reluctantly shower. There's a fine, yellow crust in the folds under my armpits, in my belly button, and in other unmentionable damp and humid places on my body. The crusty skin hurts to scrub and smells when I scratch at it. My scalp feels tender as I shampoo my hair, and big clumps tear out through my fingers when I rinse. I really need to see about changing my birth control or getting a prescription for some iron pills or something. Maybe I have some kind of thyroid issue or a fungus. Either way, I feel disgusting, like I just want to hide away from the world. I'm too young to feel like I'm falling apart.

I shave and examine my pedicure, which still looks to be in pretty good condition. My fingernails, on the other hand, are awful. That's when I notice my missing pinky nail. It's not torn or broken, but completely *gone*. I wince and touch the soft pink quick that's exposed, tender, and painful to touch. When did this happen?

My reflection in the foggy bathroom mirror is almost shocking. My normally full-cheeked, heart-shaped face is slimmer, and the hollows under my eyes are darker than usual. But it's my hair that makes me gasp. My scalp shows through in stark patches at my natural part. I don't know how, but I must have shed more hair in the shower than I realized. That does it. After this weekend with George, I'm *definitely* seeing a doctor. I'll suck it up and borrow money from my mother if I have to. But for now, I need to get to work.

I fight back tears and finish getting ready for my date. Thankfully, the creepy lady from the night before dropped my Brittany wig behind the dumpster, so I'll have something to cover up my thinning hair. It feels sketchy using the wig after it was left in the dirt behind everyone's trash, but it's my best wig and the only one George has seen me in. Maybe the woman was just bringing the wig back to me? More likely, she was doing something weird to it. Either way, I don't have much choice other than to use it. I pick out the leaves, give it a shake, and mount it on my wig stand for styling.

I dress and apply my makeup in slow motion. It takes three tries for me to properly glue on my eyelashes without them looking wonky. The tremors in my hand make it so that I can't get my eyeliner right, so I say fuck it and forget making a perfect winged look. Whatever bug I caught or thyroid condition I've suddenly developed is kicking my ass big time. I just want to rest, but I can't afford to say no to George. If I make sure he has a good time, I'll be able to get to a doctor, and everything will be fine. I'm sure.

I grab my purse, my phone charger, and my weekend bag and head down the stairs toward my car. Halfway down, I get winded and nearly tumble headfirst down the stairs. I decide that it isn't safe for me to drive and call a cab instead. I'm dizzy, and it dawns on me that I forgot to eat breakfast again. I could go into the house and eat some of Elaine's food, but I don't want to give her another reason to be angry with me. I'll be eating lunch with George soon anyway, so I decide to hold out a little longer.

I shouldn't waste money on cab fare, but I'm too exhausted to drive anywhere. In this state, I might crash into something or get pulled over by a cop or worse. I sit on the stairs and stare at the dumpster as I wait for my cab to arrive. A sick feeling worms into my gut as I remember the way the woman hissed at me before leaping into the air like a video game superhero. Normal people would have called the cops by now, but this wasn't a normal situation. Besides, what would I say? Some strange woman followed me out of the mall and stole my wig, then stalked me outside my home, then *flew* away? I would get Baker Acted in a heartbeat. At the very least, my complaint would tie me back to the mall where I did my best shoplifting. If Winona Ryder got busted and charged with grand theft, they would surely throw the book at someone like me.

My cab driver arrives and is an older man who, with a different financial background, could have been one of my daddies. He gives me a strange look when I tell him my destination, eyeing me up and down. He holds his nose and cracks a window before pulling away from my apartment. We ride in silence during the short distance to the hotel, and I pay him with the last few dollars from George and a stack of quarters I had stashed away in my sock drawer. Before I leave, he grasps my hand and stares back at me with milky eyes.

"Lady, are you okay?"

I yank my hand from his grasp. "I'm *fine*."

"You don't look so hot," he says. "Do you need some help or somethin'?"

"No." I grab my overnight bag and open the cab door. "Mind your own fucking business."

I close the cab door with a satisfying slam and immediately regret it. Just getting out of the cab took a bit of energy, and slamming the door made the muscles in my arm scream. I stand in the shade of the hotel valet parking overhang and check my messages. There's a text from an unknown number, but I have an idea who it's from.

Leo and I are together now, and you need to accept that. We have a baby and a life. You need to leave us alone, or I'll make you regret it.

"Ha!" I shout out loud to no one but myself. Leo's fiancée must have gotten a new phone number. Who the fuck does she think she is? My fingers mash into the number pad, and I furiously text.

Me? Check his phone, he's the one who—

I begin to type back an acidic response when George's car pulls up in front of the hotel. I give him my best smile, slip my phone back into my purse, and smooth the skirt of my dress. Retaliation will have to wait. For now, it's time to work.

Chapter Eight

George is unusually quiet as we drive toward the country club. He doesn't reach over to grab my hand, doesn't compliment me about my appearance, doesn't ask me about my day. Like the cab driver, he cracks the window and we ride in silence. We don't drive for long before he pulls into a Chili's Bar & Grill and parks.

"Uh, what are we doing here?" I ask. "I didn't think you were a fan of chain restaurants."

"Oh, I love their baby back ribs," he says. "Just thought we would do something different for a change."

"Okay." I shrug and haul my body out of the car.

George does not open the car door for me like usual. He doesn't take my arm as we enter the restaurant either, and in my weakened state, I could definitely use the support. In fact, he walks ahead of me and doesn't even hold the restaurant door. He lights up when we are greeted by the young, pretty hostess, however. The teen behind the host stand blinks with surprise as her gaze darts from me to George and back again.

"Welcome to Chili's," she chirps. "Table for two?"

"Do you have a table outside?" he asks.

"Certainly." The hostess grabs two menus and motions for us to follow. "Right this way."

We trail the hostess through the dining room to the deserted outdoor patio where she sits us at a rickety metallic bistro table. The patio overlooks a drainage canal and a mini-mall with a Dollar Tree and a Payless Shoes store. She hands us laminated menus and tells us our server will be out in a moment. George sighs, pulls out his reading glasses, and begins to eye the specials. I'm not even hungry, but I have a feeling George will want me to order the flight of mini desserts served in shot glasses.

"George?" I rub my foot against his under the table. He doesn't return the gesture. "Everything okay?"

George puts his menu down and removes his glasses. "Not really."

"What's up? Is it work? The house?"

"No. Frankly, it's you," he says. "Brittany, I'm worried about you."

I blink. "What do you mean? I'm fine."

"When was the last time you took a bath?"

"Excuse me?" I scoff. "I took a shower this morning before you picked me up."

George sighs and purses his lips together. A trickle of sweat slides down his temple and onto his cheek before landing on the lapel of his crisp white Ralph Lauren polo. He opens his mouth to speak, pauses, then starts again.

"It's just that you don't look very good. And you smell…unwell."

"What?"

My lower lip quivers, and a moment of silence passes between us. Before either of us can speak again, a server comes out to take our drink order. George orders an unsweetened tea and a platter of baby back ribs and fries. I'm so angry that I order the Buy One Get One Free presidente margaritas. I don't even know if I like margaritas, but my nerves are shot, and I can sense that something bad is about to happen.

"Margaritas?" George asks. "Since when do you drink?"

"Since now." I need to fix this thing between us. I smile and reach across the table, grabbing his hands. "I know that I've been a little off. I'm sorry, Daddy. I just haven't been feeling well. But I'll be better, I promise."

George glances down at my hand. I forgot that I was missing a pinky nail. He makes a disgusted expression and pulls away.

"It's not just that," he says. "This isn't working out anymore."

"Oh."

My shoulders slump. Here it comes: the breakup. George may not have paid me the most of all my daddies, but he's one of the kindest and easiest to get along with. Tears spring to my eyes as I realize I won't be able to pay Elaine this month's rent after all.

"You're a lovely girl, Brittany," he says. "But I think it's best if we don't see each other anymore."

I nod and wipe the wetness from my eyes. Desperation flutters in my chest, beating against my ribcage like a terrified bird with a broken wing. The server delivers our drinks, and I down the first margarita straight from the shaker in one gulp. The alcohol burns my throat and floods my veins with the confidence I needed all at once. I slam the plastic margarita shaker on the table and stare into George's stunned eyes. Some primal, animalistic part of me bubbles to the surface, hot and frothy, a part of me that's always lurking just beneath the skin. I open my mouth and let the venom spill from my lips.

"Five thousand dollars."

George chokes and spits out his tea. "Excuse me?"

"You wanna break up? Fine," I say. "But it's going to cost you five thousand dollars."

"Now, Brittany." He chuckles. "It doesn't have to be like that—"

"Actually, it does," I say, pulling out my phone. "In fact, it's a pretty modest price to pay for my silence."

"You little cunt." He chuckles again and wipes the sweat from his brow. "I'm not paying you anything."

"I'll scream," I say. "I'll scream right fucking now. Everyone in the restaurant will look at you. You think you can hide with me out here on the patio? They'll see. They'll know what a piece of shit you are."

"Who do you think you are to threaten me—"

"HELP!" I screech and stand up from the table. The metallic chair scrapes against the concrete and crashes to the ground with a teeth-rattling clang. "AHHHHHH!"

George's tanned complexion pales, and his mouth hangs open as I continue to scream. It doesn't take long for our server to bolt out onto the patio, panting and frantic.

"Is everything okay?" the server asks. "Ma'am?"

I stare George down with my craziest, most wild-eyed look. He finally understands what he's up against. *Who* he's up against.

"Yes, there wa-was…a wasp. A wasp bu-bu-buzzing around." George stammers and swallows. "It's gone now."

My crazed expression melts into a satisfied grin. I lift my chair off the ground, sit down, and give the server a reassuring smile. "Sorry. I thought I was going to get stung."

The server's gaze flicks back and forth between George and I. Satisfied, they nod and retreat. "Okay, well, just let me know if you need anything else."

"Thank you," I say, sweet as pie.

When the server is gone, George leans back in his chair and lets out a long, loud sigh.

"Okay," he says. "You proved your point. Now what?"

"Now, we come to a resolution. One that's mutually beneficial, of course."

"Of course." George grumbles and reaches for his wallet. "How much?"

"Five," I say, "thousand."

"Fuck that." He chuckles. "One."

"Fine. I'll just text everyone in my phone book your name. Along with the location of your law practice and the fact that you love jerking off to feet."

"Psh," George chuckles. "Go for it. No one is going to believe you and your little friends."

"I'm sure they'll believe their own eyes," I say. "I have quite a few interesting photos of you with my shoes. What would your law partners think? Or your wife?"

George stares at me from across the table, fists clenched as if he's daring me. His eyes are cold, but the red patches creeping up his neck into his jowls betray him. Up until now, I've played it demure and calm for him. He paid for me to act the part of a passive pushover, someone he could manipulate and suppress. An object for him to use. Well, I'm not on his payroll anymore.

"Five thousand dollars and I go away quietly," I say. "You'll never see or hear from me again."

George sighs and nods. "Alright."

"Today," I say. "You need to pay me today, or no deal."

"Brittany, I can't just get you five thousand dollars," he says. "The banks are closed after noon on the weekend."

"Write me a check then."

"A check will trace me back to you." He opens his wallet and thumbs through a stack of cash. He counts it, puts half back in his wallet, and gives half to me. "That's $800. I can get the rest for you on Monday."

I frown and count the money. "Fine."

"Fine."

The server returns with George's food, and I suck down my second margarita. He asks the server for a to-go box and the check, and we sit in silence staring at the parking lot. I'm still seething, but I also can't help but feel a little triumphant. Five thousand bucks isn't much in the grand scheme of things, but it's enough to set me up until I figure out what I want to do with my life. Maybe this is for the best. Maybe this is my sign that it's time to shake things up and do something different. Something that makes me happier than scraping by all the time.

George pays for our meal, and we leave the restaurant. I

wait near the front door and pull out my phone as George walks ahead of me. He turns around and gives me an annoyed expression as I struggle to mash the keypad on my phone.

"What are you doing?" he asks. "Let's go."

"I'm calling a cab," I say. "I'm not getting in a car with you."

"Fucking, goddamn," George mutters and walks away.

"Bye, Daddy!" I call after him. "See you Monday!"

George slams his car door and peels away from Chili's as I look on, triumphant. I order the cab, and as I wait for my ride, an elderly couple exits the building. They give me a strange look as they walk toward their car. I bare my teeth and hiss at them.

A few moments later, a different cab driver arrives and regards me with disgust, just like all the others. I get in and tell him the address of my apartment. I feel lighter somehow as the cab driver takes me back home. I lean against the window and smile, picking at my remaining pinky nail, not at all disturbed by how loose it is against the quick. We're almost to my apartment when a surge of power rips through my veins. Standing up to George gave me a sense of self-esteem and purpose that I hadn't experienced in a long, long time. I may be falling apart on the outside, but inside, I have a newfound strength.

I sit up, and the skin on my forehead peels away from the window, leaving a trail of sticky, stringy, slug-like matter. My forehead impression on the glass is thick and putrid-smelling, and I smile at the notion that I'm marking my territory. I lower the window, take off my wig, and throw it out of the moving car.

RIP Brittany.

Chapter Nine

The first thing I do when I get home is peel off five hundred-dollar bills and slide them under Elaine's bedroom door. The second thing I do is flop on my bed and turn on the television. Margarita sloshes in my belly, and I lie in a drunken haze, curling up in my bed until sleep takes me.

When I wake up later, there's a note from Elaine on the table.

Thanks for the rent. I still think we should talk later.
Truly worried about you.
- E

I toss the note back on the counter, conflicted. I've been a shit to Elaine. I can self-reflect enough to admit that it's because I'm jealous of her. She's got a good career. She's smart with her money. She has a cool girlfriend who loves her. What do I have? A borderline alcoholic mother, a shoplifting addiction, and an unhealthy obsession with my ex. Elaine deserves better than to have me as a friend and roommate. It's a good thing she's moving out. I would only keep dragging her down.

My stomach yells at me for food as I eye the refrigerator. The only thing I've consumed all day was two cheap margaritas. Now that I have some cash again, I know I should buy groceries instead of heading to the mall or the drive-through. I grab my reusable grocery totes from the hallway closet and begin to make a mental shopping list. See? I can be responsible. I can be capable of growth.

It's getting dark outside, and my nap has rejuvenated me enough so that I feel like I can drive again. A new cold front must have come through because I'm freezing, so I put on my warmest coat—a faux fur George got me for Christmas—to wear to the grocery store. The sun is setting, but the light still hurts my eyes, so I have to dig out my sunglasses.

I used to enjoy driving, but now it seems like such a chore. The air conditioner and heater on my piece of crap car stopped working long ago and the dashboard is beginning to crack and rot from exposure to the sun. I've had this car since high school, and even though it was never new, back then it didn't feel so worn out. I used to drive my friends all around town listening to our favorite CDs with the window rolled down, the breeze in my hair. I felt free. That girl didn't know how shitty life was going to be, how just riding around in a used car with your friends and listening to music was as good as it was ever going to get. God, how depressing.

Maybe some music will help lift my spirits now. At a stoplight, I pull out my CD wallet from beneath the car seat. It's covered in sand, and I can't remember the last time I even cracked it open. I flip through the pages of CDs, plastic inserts crusted together with spilled soda and grime, and find my treasured Sundays album. I played it over and over again after a particularly bad breakup in high school when I just wanted to wallow in my sadness. I pop the album into the CD player and wait for Harriet Wheeler's haunting voice to soothe me, but nothing comes out. The LCD screen flashes ERROR at me as the disc spins and spins inside the player.

"Sonofabitch!" I ball my hand into a fist and bring it down on the CD player. Then I bring it down again. And again.

ERROR.
ERROR.
ERROR.

I take a deep breath and realize that beating the shit out of my radio will not produce the effects I'm looking for. Fine. No music. I'll just be sad in silence instead. All my little outburst managed to do was hurt my hand and probably lose my CD inside the player forever.

After I pull into the grocery store and park, I finally get a good look at my hands. There's a gash on my knuckles from where I punched my radio, and another fingernail is missing. Upon further inspection, the gash is much worse than I initially thought. The skin is completely gone, revealing dried-out sinew and muscle and a flash of white bone. Despite the dramatic-looking cut on my hand, somehow, I'm not bleeding. I rummage through my purse and cover the wound up with a bandage, trying not to freak out. Why isn't there any blood?

Despite my best efforts, I can't stop myself from crying, though the sobs come without tears. I'm normally a great crier. When I was a kid, I even learned to cry on demand just like an actress. So, where are the tears now? When I've worked the last sob out of my system, I take off my sunglasses and flip down the visor to inspect my face. My reflection isn't great. Dark half moons shadow the underside of my bloodshot eyes, one of which is colored with more red than white. The eyebrow above my left eye also looks suspiciously thinner. I rub at the eyebrow with my fingertip, and dark brow hairs fall into my lap like snowflakes. I slip my oversized sunglasses on and try to be brave as I leave the safety of my shitty car for the grocery store.

My shoulders feel so heavy that I have to hunch over as I walk through the automatic double doors. I use my shopping cart for support as I push it down the aisles, leaning over the handle and using the buggy to propel me. I should have gotten a motorized cart instead. I feel decrepit and dried out like the Crypt Keeper as I head toward the vitamin aisle. I need better nutrition, that's definitely part of my problem. A girl can't live off of mall takeout alone. I grab a bottle of women's multivitamins, a prenatal vitamin, glucosamine, chondroitin, vitamin C, vitamin D, calcium. I should have thought of this before. What I need is fresh fruit, sunshine, activity, and healthy living. I can dig myself out of this hole. I have to.

In the produce section, my hand brushes against the hand of another woman as we both reach for the bananas. She makes a sound of surprise, laughs, and turns to me.

"I'm so sorry—" the woman gasps, stops dead in her tracks. She's about the same age as my mother, conservatively dressed and plump with a Hillary Clinton hairdo. She doesn't even try to be discreet as her gaze trails up and down my body.

"Something the matter?" I smile, glance at the bunches of bananas, and pluck a pink and white disc from the pile. "Oops. Lost another nail."

The woman manages a tight-lipped smile and walks away. Before the last few days, an interaction like that would have left me feeling hurt and sad. Insecure. Instead, I felt powerful. My very existence clearly disgusted the woman, just like I had disgusted George and my cab drivers. I liked it. They all think I'm disgusting for living the way I do anyway. They may as well get the full, visceral experience of me.

I load my shopping cart with bagged salads, fresh-cut fruit, yogurt, skim milk, lean meats, and sparkling artesian water. Low-carb bread and high-protein shakes. I also grab containers of pre-made green gelatin snack packs for my client's photo shoot. I'm determined to feel good again, inside and out, no matter what it takes. I have to keep working, and I have to try to take better care of myself. I can be a healthier, stronger person—the person I used to be—if I just stop acting like a victim or a doormat all the time. I know I can.

My cashier is a fresh-scrubbed teenager with a blonde cheerleader ponytail. She greets me with an upbeat, customer service greeting and smile, but quickly changes her tune as she meets my bloodshot gaze. I hunch over the conveyor belt and slowly unload the groceries from my cart, coughing little red-tinged sprays of spittle onto my hand as I work. When she's finished ringing me up, the cashier regards me with terror as I hand her the last of the money from George. I hiss farewell to her and leave the grocery store with less than forty dollars and a trunk full of aspirational groceries that will surely change my life.

When I return home, my parking lot is cloaked in night. I warily eye the dumpster, half expecting my bug-eyed stalker to be looming behind a pile of trash bags, ready to strike at me again. As I lug the first bag of groceries upstairs, it becomes clear I woefully overestimated my energy levels. I go back down for the rest and am barely able to move by the time I finish putting my groceries away.

I make myself a cup of tea and a bowl of yogurt with nuts, berries, and granola and retreat to my bedroom. Even though I cleaned the day before, the room still stinks like dirty socks or funky, unwashed gym clothes. I click on the television, and Paris Hilton and Nicole Richie appear on the screen doing their dumb heiress act. I witness them prance around the countryside in skimpy pink outfits as I eat my yogurt and zone out.

Tomorrow. I just have to get through tomorrow, and then on Monday, I will go see George and collect the rest of the money he promised me. I'll figure out the rest after that. Tomorrow, I'll go see my mother and have her help me find a doctor to figure out what's going on with my body. And Elaine. I would make things right with Elaine, too. It was the least she deserved.

I lay back in bed and let my eyes glaze over, hypnotized by the TV glow. I fall asleep to the lullaby of a laugh track, content in my sweaty bed sheet cocoon, but my bladder wakes me in the middle of the night. My hair is matted to the back of my neck in a sweaty nest, and my joints scream with a hot, pulsing pain. I relieve myself in the bathroom, and a hot stream of horrible-smelling urine hits the bowl. I barely find the strength to hobble to the kitchen and chase four ibuprofen with a liter of water.

I'm fully awake and edgy when I return to my bedroom. I'm behind on my work but in no state to answer emails or entertain clients. It's a mistake to open my laptop, but I do it anyway. My unanswered emails stare back at me, and I remember the photos that I had promised to my foot fetish clients. Fuck. I return to the kitchen and retrieve a large rectangular tub from under the sink, as well as the green gelatin cups from the fridge. Might as well get this over with.

Back in my bedroom, I rip open the lids on the plastic containers and turn the cartons upside down into a big plastic vat. The gelatin makes a slippery suction noise before releasing from its encasement and plopping into the tub with a splat. I repeat this until all of the gelatin cups are empty and the tub is full of wobbling lime goo. Then I turn on my digital camera, stick my feet in the tub of cold green jelly, and fire away.

SNAP.

SNAP.

SNAP.

I take about a dozen photos of my feet and toes squished into the gelatinous tub before I review my work. I can't say that I understand the draw of this particular thing, but I try not to judge my clients when it comes to kink. I don't get why gelatin and feet are sexual, but this type of thing isn't hurting anyone, and at the end of the day, I'm just happy to be paid. I review the shots I took and admit they turned out okay, except, upon further inspection, something seems off. I zoom in on a photo of my left foot and gasp. My eyes dart to the tub of quivering jelly, and a sick feeling invades my gut.

No. *Nononononono.*

I plunge my hands into the cold muck and pull out a single pinky toe.

Chapter Ten

The sun is rising as I bundle up in my coat and fly down the stairs in a flurry of fur and panic. My pinky toe is in my pocket, wrapped in a plastic baggie and nestled on a bed of ice. I don't have much hope for it being reattached. The little nub is gray and looks like it probably lost its blood supply long ago. I've tried to ignore my failing health or shrug off what has been happening as no big deal for too long. I can't go to a walk-in clinic or wait for my mother to help me find a specialist. The emergency room is the only sane solution now.

Dawn rays of light assault my eyes as I drive out of the apartment complex parking lot toward the ER. I slip my sunglasses on again, but they barely do anything to tone down the glare. My thoughts are all over the place as I swerve in and out of traffic like a demented Cruella de Vil. What kind of virus or disease could I possibly have that would cause my toe to fall off? Diabetes? Not likely. Maybe it's leprosy? The thought makes my stomach drop. What if I got infected somehow by that weird woman who assaulted me? Did she give me fucking *leprosy*?

I make it all the way to the emergency room parking lot before my chest caves in and a panic attack sets in. I grip the steering wheel and squeeze my eyes shut, trying to ground myself again. When I was younger, right before my parents divorced, I would often have panic attacks that left me frozen, terrified, and stuck inside myself. My mother would sit with me and teach me how to focus on my breath, in through the nose, out through the mouth. I forget everything she taught me as I clench the wheel, panting, breathing in and out in short, sharp breaths.

After a few minutes, my pulse and heart rate slow. I realize that I haven't even looked at the wound site where my toe detached. The truth is that I'm too scared to look. But I want to know what I'm up against before I walk through those emergency room doors.

I pull my left knee up to my chest and slip out of the ballet flats I put on before I left the apartment, followed by the ankle sock. I don't feel any pain at the sight of the injury, though I attribute that fact to adrenaline doing its job. I close my eyes, take a deep breath, and peek down at the place where my pinky toe used to be and...

Nothing.

Nada. Just smooth, closed-up skin and an empty place where a digit used to be. I blink and run my fingertips along the unmarked skin and let out a blast of laughter.

What the fuck is going on?

Just to be sure, I pull the pinky toe bag from my pocket and examine the contents inside. Tears well up, and a stray droplet falls down my cheek as I realize nothing will ever be the same again. Well, at least I can cry again. Even if I go inside the hospital, the doctors probably can't sew my toe back on. It was already gray and rotten-looking when I pulled it from the vat of gelatin, so who knows how long it had been like that. Plus, the way that the closed-off skin on my foot looks makes it seem like the wound healed ages ago. The emergency room staff would just think I was nuts and send me home with a huge hospital bill. Doctors can't help me, and I don't know how to help myself. I wipe the tears from my eyes, stick the toe baggie back in my pocket, and throw my car in reverse.

On the way home, I pass by Bay Vistas Condominium. A wave of anger floods over me as I mull over the events of the last few days and my ruined foot. Even if I wanted to continue the sugar baby/foot fetish business, it would be much harder with only nine toes. Sure, there were plenty of niche buyers out there who would be into that sort of thing, but I don't want to be niche. I want my fucking toe.

I was doing fine until that weird fucking woman came into my life, just fine. Healthy as a horse! I *must* have contracted some strange, unknown virus from her or something; it's the only logical answer. If that's the case, going to the emergency room won't be enough anyway. I need answers. I need vengeance. I need to make that bitch pay.

My tires screech against the asphalt as I do a U-turn and head back toward Bay Vista Condominiums. I don't know which building that horrible woman lives in, but I know that she has a shitty little dog. And like all shitty little dogs, hers probably has to pee a thousand times a day. That's not fair. It's probably a nice little dog who just has a terrible owner. The dog didn't deserve my anger. But still! All I have to do is wait until she takes the dog out for its morning walk, and then I can follow her and find out which condo is hers.

I pull into Bay Vista and park in my usual visitors' spot, sink down low in my seat, and angle the rearview mirror to get a good look at the sidewalk. She passed by me with her little dog in this very same spot before, so there was no reason to believe she wouldn't walk by again. I shudder remembering her sneer at me on that first day. It was the same look of revulsion she had for me in the glow of my headlights in the mall parking. The same look on her shadowy face behind the dumpster. The face of disgust and disease and rot.

Bad thoughts invade my mind as I wait for my stalker to emerge from whatever hellhole she crawls out of. What if I lose more than a few fingernails and some hair and a toe? What if my ears fall off next, or my nose? What if this was just the beginning of something far worse? Before I can ponder too many other horrible possibilities or terrible fates, a flurry of fur and hair catches my attention.

It's her.

The woman stands at the outskirts of the condominium property with a leash in one hand and a smoldering cigarette in the other. In the early dawn light, she doesn't look as terrifying as before. In fact, she looks...better. Younger. If it weren't for the coat, sunglasses, and Yorkie on the other end of the leash, I would almost doubt it was her.

The little dog does its business, and I hold still in my hiding position until the woman walks away. When she's just about to turn the corner, I open my car door and walk at a brisk pace to follow behind her. Despite missing one toe and feeling completely decrepit, I'm surprisingly fast on my feet. I hide around the corner of the main condo building and watch as she enters the Bay Vista Condominiums vestibule. Through the tinted glass windows, I watch her punch the number nine on the elevator panel.

There's a card key entry to get into the vestibule, but I don't have to wait long for someone else to walk through the door. A well-to-do middle-aged couple takes their time exiting the building, giving me the perfect opportunity to slip in behind them. My heart jackhammers in my ears as I push the number nine and step into the empty elevator.

As the elevator goes up, up, up, it occurs to me that I don't know which condo belongs to the woman, only that she rode up to the ninth floor. When the elevator doors open, I don't have to do much guessing. The ninth floor is the top floor and, by default, has the only condo on the floor—the penthouse. This lady must be loaded.

I tread as softly as I can across the carpet toward a set of white French double doors marked 901. The muffled sound of a yipping Yorkie greets me through the closed doors, and panic sets in again. I came here to confront this woman, but I don't really have a plan. I'm not a violent person, so I don't want to hurt her. I just want to get some answers, and probably to cuss at her. But before I can chicken out and turn around, one of the French doors swings open wide, and I'm staring down the barrel of a shotgun.

I don't breathe, don't speak, don't move a muscle as the

woman lowers her weapon. She frowns, places her oversized sunglasses on top of her forehead, and stares me down with a pair of deep violet eyes.

"Oh, it's you." She sighs and picks up her little dog. "Well, don't just stand there. You might as well come in."

Chapter Eleven

"I suppose you're here for answers or revenge or some other such nonsense," she says, closing the door behind me. "Can I get you a coffee? Water? Tea?"

I blink and let my eyes adjust in the poorly lit dungeon of a condo. My nose twitches as the scent of dog and something familiar hits my nostrils. Dust. Dirty laundry. Decay. I shouldn't be here. Every instinct in my body says to run as far away as possible from this woman. Before I give myself a chance to turn around and escape, I remember why I bothered to find her in the first place. I needed answers, and I was going to get them.

"I don't need a drink. I need to know what you did to me."

I stand in the doorway, not yet ready to venture further. The woman places her little dog on the floor, sighs, and walks toward the kitchen.

"Oh, don't be so dramatic," she says. "Come this way."

Her heels click against the polished marble floor, and she

disappears around the corner. The little dog looks up at me before trailing behind its mistress. After a moment's deliberation, I follow her toward the kitchen with my fists still clenched.

Despite the generous, open floor plan and floor-to-ceiling windows, the space is cave-like and not at all decorated like a luxury beachfront property. Heavy cranberry colored velvet drapery covers every single window, and all of the shades are drawn, blocking out the light. Instead of coastal rattan furniture in light colors and breezy fabrics, the decor is heavy and dark. The credenza in the entryway is crafted of dark mahogany wood, intricately carved and enormous, with a dining room set to match. The still life paintings, landscapes, and portraits on the wall are all old-fashioned with elaborate gilded frames, scenes of proud lords and ladies, and their stately countryside homes. This lady didn't get the memo that Florida condos were supposed to be filled with seashells and tropical motifs. This place looks more like an 18th-century European manor.

I round the corner to the kitchen, which is also similarly old-fashioned looking, all wood and cast iron and dark marble. The woman stands next to a monstrous-looking black wrought iron range that certainly didn't come standard in the apartment. The oven seems big enough to cook a whole person in, and the range top is evil and Gothic-looking with twisting, heavy black wrought iron. She pours a cup of dark liquid from a silver teapot and turns to me without smiling.

"I already made coffee," the woman says, shoving a cup in my hand. "You should have some. Looks like you need it."

"Your house is weird." I sniff the cup. "How do I know it isn't poisoned?"

"Muh huh, mwa ha HA HA!" A ridiculous laugh bursts from the woman's lips.

I frown at her and put the cup on the marble slab counter.

"Oh, honey, if I wanted you dead, you already would be," she says. "Go ahead. Drink your coffee. It's good shit, single-sourced. Not that crap from the grocery store."

She takes a sip of her coffee, smacks her lips, and makes an *ahhhh* sound of satisfaction. "You want to know why I've been following you, right?"

"Well, for starters, yeah," I say. "Did you *do* something to me?"

"Yes and no," she says. "I was following you because you have potential."

"I don't get it."

"I see girls like you all the time," she says. "Young. Pretty. And too stupid to know their own worth."

"Listen, lady, if I did something to piss you off or whatever, then I'm sorry." I pull the baggie from my pocket and wave it in the air. "But my fucking *toe* fell off this morning, and I'm kind of freaked out. So tell me what you did to me, or…or I'll call the cops!"

The woman eyes the bag, *tsks*, and shakes her head. "Well, that *is* a shame."

"It's not a *shame*, it's my life! Now tell me what the fuck is going on!"

The woman sighs and leans against her counter. She looks so small and frail against the monstrous kitchen appliance. I'm so furious I could choke her—wrap my fingers around her pale, slim neck, and squeeze until her stupid purple eyeballs burst out of the socket like those squishy toys you get at the arcade. But I don't have the energy, and I'm on her turf, and besides, she has information I need. This awful woman has the upper hand, and I hate it.

"Before our *interaction,* you were perfectly happy wasting your talents in favor of spending time with awful men who didn't properly value you. True?"

"How do you know that?"

"I've been following you for a while," she says. "You're a good artist, by the way. A terrible thief, but a good artist. You should really keep that up, the painting."

"Okay, so you're a weirdo stalker. Why is my life and what I do any of your business?"

"Because you're squandering your existence away. Your beautiful life energy. Well, I certainly wasn't going to let it go to waste."

"I'm not wasting my life," I say, insulted. "I have ambitions. I have goals. It's hard to make it out there in the world, you know?"

"You just let those men debase you, over and over again…"

"But that was my choice," I say. "And they didn't debase me. My clients were never the ones who hurt me. They always treated me well. It was…"

"It was what?"

"Well, you supposedly stalked me and know everything about my life," I say. "Don't you know?"

"I do," she says. "But I want to hear you say it."

I blink and lick my lips. My mouth is made of cotton, and I don't want to say his name, but I say it anyway. "Leo."

"What about him?"

I shift on my feet and stare at her vaulted ceilings. My body aches even worse than usual, and I'm on the verge of tears again. What the fuck good was any of this going to do?

"Listen, lady, I don't need a therapy session. I need you to help me feel better again. I have clients! I have a life. I need to get back to work, so can we just wrap this up, please?"

"Tell me what happened and I'll help you."

I laugh and stare at my feet. Nine toes. Soon I'll only have eight. Then seven, then…

"Fine." I sniff, wipe my eyes, and square my shoulders. "After he left and moved to Brooklyn without me, I… I guess I just gave up."

"Gave up?"

I shrug. "Yeah. I stopped taking care of myself. I just didn't want to live anymore, I guess."

"You let yourself go," the woman snored. "All for a man with bad facial hair and terrible taste in art."

"I didn't let myself go," I hiss. "I'm depressed. *Fuck*."

"Well. Go on."

"I suppose you already know," I say. "After a few months, I was going to move there to be with him. I stayed back to finish one last gallery showing downtown, and then the plan was for me to relocate."

I pause, take a deep, shuddering breath. I haven't spoken to anyone about this out loud. Not Elaine. Not my mother. Whenever anyone asks if I want to talk about it, I just change the topic. Shove it down. It was too hard to talk about it. Too embarrassing. Too painful.

"Why didn't you move to Brooklyn to live with your boyfriend?"

A tear rolls down my cheek. I shake my head and hug my arms to my chest. My heart feels like it could burst through my ribcage, crack open, and leap from my chest just like the creature from Alien.

"Because a week before my gallery showing, he called me and said he was with someone else." I smile through closed lips, shake my head again. "And that she was pregnant, and they were going to get married."

The woman regards me with something akin to sympathy. The expression looks strange played out on her sharp features, her usually smug lips coiled into a look of disgust.

"You threw it all away and let yourself rot."

I laugh. "Yeah. I guess I did."

"I saw that rot, when I looked into your eyes," she says, eyebrows raised. "You're a talented artist, but you let it go. Why?"

"I guess I just couldn't hack it anymore. I canceled my gallery showing, destroyed every one of my paintings, and lay in bed for a month. I got fired from my job. I didn't feel like seeing friends or going out anymore. I needed to make money, so I got back into foot modeling and started meeting daddies."

"Does your new line of work pay well?"

"It should," I say. "I know other girls get paid more than I do. I never know what to charge for my time."

"You're a beautiful young woman. You should really value yourself more, you know."

The impromptu therapy session was beginning to annoy me.

"Listen, lady," I say. "Whatever you did to me, just undo it, okay? Right fucking now, or I'll call the cops, I mean it."

"And tell them what?" She chuckles, low and deep. "That I made your toe fall off?"

"That you were stalking me!"

"While you were shoplifting from the mall?" She smirks. "Not a good look for you. Besides, what makes you think they'll believe you?"

"Fuck!" I run my hands through my hair in frustration. A big clump of hair tears through my fingers, taking another fingernail with it. A lump settles in my throat, and I start crying again like a big baby as I hold out a handful of my hair to her. "Please. Please, you have to make this stop."

"What's done is done," she says. "I can't take it back from the one who made me like this any more than you can. But I can show you how to feel a little better. Come, follow me."

I'm fully sobbing as I follow this strange woman down a hallway toward a series of rooms with closed doors. I am so desperate for answers and for help that I ignore all of my stranger danger instincts. I hate this woman and I want to hurt her, but for now, she's the only lead I have for getting back to normal.

"It's so much easier these days to capture an image, you know?" She says, opening the last door on the left. "Back in my day, I had to commission an artist to paint a portrait for me, and well, you know how long that takes. And what talent!"

I wipe my eyes, and a trail of eyelashes comes off on the

back of my hand. "Do you always speak in riddles? I'm losing my eyelashes now. God, I really can't afford to get extensions."

She enters the room, and I follow, half-expecting to be led into some sort of torture chamber or sex dungeon. Maybe this is where she brings her victims to bleed them dry. Maybe I'll never leave this luxury waterfront condo again. As I enter the room, I see that it's not a creepy prison, but a studio. An art studio. Every inch of the wall is covered in paintings, illustrations, and photos of beautiful young women from every corner of the world.

"Who are they?" I ask.

The woman walks toward a weathered square-shaped photo from the 1970s and strokes it with a wan hand. The woman in the picture has red hair and wears a crochet halter top, her features too blurred for me to make out.

"These are my beauties," she says. "Women like you, who won't be missed."

Anger fizzes between my ears. "That's a fucked up thing to say."

"Do you remember the night at the mall?" She turns to face me, crossing her arms at her chest.

I blink, the memory of that night still fresh in my mind. The flash of light. Snap. Whiz. It made sense now. "You took my photo that night, didn't you?"

"Of course."

"You also stole my favorite wig."

"I returned it to you," she says.

"Thanks, I guess?"

"To be fair, I didn't know it was a wig. I needed a hair

sample, that's all. Thankfully, there were a few strands of your real hair inside the wig."

"Seriously, can you just get to the point…"

"The night I took your photo was the night that your energy became *my* energy." She nods to the far side of the room, where an entire section of wall is covered in Polaroid photos. "I suppose these days I could use one of those phones to take a photo, but I quite like having a physical copy of the image."

I walk over to the wall of Polaroid photos, some of them yellowed and faded, by the looks of them dating back to before I was born. In each photo is a surprised-looking young woman, her features partially blurred and obscured. I survey the room, noticing that all the other photographs and portraits have blurred features too.

"Where's my photo?"

The woman lets out another dark chuckle. "I'm sure you'd like to know. I'm keeping it somewhere safe. For now."

"Give it back!"

"No. Besides, it won't help you."

"So let me have it then," I demand. "I never gave you permission to photograph me. I control my image—I control who gets access to me!"

The woman gives me another condescending smile. I want to choke her. We stare each other down as I assess my situation. I know I don't have the strength to take her.

"Do you want my help or not?" she asks.

I pause. Do I? At this point, it doesn't seem as though I have any other choice but to take her help. If she did this to me, it made sense that she would know how to undo it, too.

"Yes."

"I chose you because of this fighting spirit you're showing me right now," she says. "It takes guts to come here, to face me like this. Unfortunately, most of them don't. So I'm going to reward you if you're willing to go all the way."

Am I willing to go all the way? Some days I'm not even willing to get out of bed. At this moment, I'm desperate, and know if I don't do something soon, an appendage I'm sure to miss will rot off my body next.

"Yes," I say. "What do I need to do?"

The woman smiles. "You need to start your own collection of beauties."

Chapter Twelve

I lose another fingernail on the drive home. My meeting with the woman didn't go the way I expected, though I suppose I didn't know what to expect. How long had this woman been preying on vulnerable women? Normal people would go to the police and report her, but this isn't a normal situation. I'm up against an energy sucking serial killer, one who can float, of all things. This isn't the kind of situation that you can ask others to help with unless you want them to think you're mad. I arrived at Bay Vista Condos scared and looking for vengeance, and instead, left confused and armed with a terrible solution to my problem.

By the time I get to the apartment, I'm exhausted and in need of sleep again. I don't want to think about what the woman told me or what she said I had to do. With every step I take, the delicate bones on the top of my feet crunch with shooting pain as if they're fracturing under my body weight. If I don't do what she says, there will only be more fractured bones and lost pieces of me. I know what I have to do, but I don't have the courage to do it. Before all this, I could never hurt someone else for my own benefit, but now, I'm not so sure.

Elaine is gone again, either at work or avoiding me at her girlfriend's place. I'm glad. I don't want to see her right now, not in this state. I chug a glass of milk over the kitchen sink and head to my rank-smelling bedroom. I'm too tired to make anything to eat, and not hungry enough to bother anyway.

I lock my door, flop on the bed, and prepare myself to rot.

With my last bit of energy, I locate the remote and click on the TV. If I'm going to decompose alive, I might as well do it with a sitcom laugh track in the background. The warm glow of electromagnetic waves and the friendly background noises of commercials and television show intros soothe me. It sucks that Elaine will have to find my rotted corpse. I wonder how long it will take for me to die. I wonder what death will be like.

The family sitcom starts with the frazzled mother calling her group of hellion sons to the dinner table. I sink further into my mattress and wonder what it would have been like if I had a big, chaotic family with multiple siblings and a two-parent household. Maybe I would have had more people to look out for me, to love me, to help me during hard times. Then again, maybe not. What is it that my mother used to say? *You made your bed, now you get to lie in it.* Right.

My skin is so sensitive now that every movement is torture against my scratchy bed sheets. I'm too tired to stand up, and it hurts too much to lie down. How much longer until I can't move or get out of bed at all? How much longer until another irreplaceable body part falls off? I'm beginning to understand why people would want to put themselves out of their own misery.

A toothpaste commercial comes on, and my tongue probes the tops and sides of my teeth. My back molars feel loose and squishy inside my gums, as though they are just floating there without long, twisting roots to anchor them to my skull. Hair and eyelashes and teeth can all be covered up and replaced, but what if I lose an ear next? Or my nose?

Power, wealth, beauty, influence. It will all be yours.

The woman didn't give me details on how this whole process worked. Was she some kind of witch? A vampire? I didn't want to know. I only want out of this hellish cycle. I want to feel like myself again. What she had to offer sounded good, of course, maybe not the power, but I could certainly use the money. Could I really go through with what she asked me to do? I don't think I have it in me.

Capture their image, consume their essence.

I shudder at the memory of the word *consume*. I picture her crouched behind my apartment complex dumpster, picking out strands of my hair from the wig and slurping them down like spaghetti. It doesn't have to be hair, though. Blood. Fingernails. Hair. Semen. She said any biological matter would do.

Stare into their eyes, claim their soul.

I don't even have to say any magic words or wait for a full moon or some shit. She didn't say what order I had to perform the ritual in, either, just that I had to take a picture of someone and keep it forever. Make eye contact with that person, then eat their hair or fingernail clippings or whatever. And then…

And then I would be back to normal again. Better than

normal, according to the woman. My hair would grow back, my skin would glow, and my body would never wither, wrinkle, or gray beyond my current age. I would attract so much wealth and have so much power that I wouldn't need to be a sugar baby or foot model anymore. I could paint all day long if I want and have a successful gallery showing without the help of all those pretentious assholes downtown. Well, they weren't all assholes, but the ones Leo was friends with were. Fuck 'em.

They will rot, and you will thrive, then they must choose to live or die.

Hours pass, and the theme music for *The Price is Right* flows through the television speakers. The last of my eyelashes flutter onto my pillowcase, and I think about my mother again. We didn't have the best relationship, but it would break her if her only child were found melted and desiccated in her bed, all gross bones and dried out beef jerky like that victim in the movie *Se7en*. I could be here in this bed for ages, slowly rotting and wasting away to nothing with only my poor mother to mourn me.

The Price is Right ends, and I hear a knock on my door.

"Hey, everything okay in there?"

Elaine's voice is softer than usual. She must not be mad at me anymore.

"Fine," I say. "Just trying to rest."

"Hey, when you're feeling better, I thought maybe we could make dinner together again," Elaine says. "We could watch a movie too. Maybe have a girls' night in?"

My lips purse together as I fight the urge to cry. My voice is squeaky, betraying me as I reply. "Sure."

"I really am worried about you," she says. "I... I think

maybe you need some help. You don't have to suffer alone, you know?"

Suffer alone. What did Elaine know about that? She had it all. It wasn't her fault, though. If I had the strength, I would get up, unlock my door, and hug her.

"I'll be fine," I say. "Thank you for checking on me."

"Okay," she says. "I'm going out for a while, but I'll be back if you need anything."

"Okay. Elaine?"

"Yeah?"

"I'm sorry I've been such an asshole."

"Don't worry about it," she says. "I just want you to be okay."

"Thank you."

Elaine sighs through the door and pads away. It's best that she doesn't see me like this. I don't want to hurt her either, and I'm worried I'll be tempted to take her photo and see if this magic spell or whatever works. Elaine doesn't deserve that, but then again, I guess no one does.

I begin to drift off again when my phone rings for the first time in days. I glance at the local number and let the call go to voicemail. I should just let the battery die along with me; let my little pink phone run down and power off for one last time, never to illuminate and cry out again. Someone leaves a voice message, and it takes all I have to reach the phone, flip it open, and play the message on speakerphone.

"Hey, it's me." Leo's voice fills my bedroom. My blood pressure elevates. "It's my mom's birthday, so I'm in town for a few days. Just me. Ahem…er, anyway. I thought maybe we could meet up for a drink. Catch up, you know. I'm still worried about you, and I want a chance to clear the air. You can call me back at this number. I'm here until Friday. Would love to see you."

BEEP.

"Yeah, I bet you would." I groan. "Fucker."

I stare at my phone and play the message again. Fucking Leo. Couldn't be faithful to me, and now he can't help himself from coming back for seconds while his fiancée and baby are waiting for him at home. Even if I was in the mood to meet up with Leo, I was in no state to do so. Maybe he really was just worried about me, but I knew enough about him and the hearts of men not to believe that it could be true. With Leo, there's always an ulterior motive, always an end game for his needs or wants.

Why should he have his cake and eat it too? He left and has everything: a family, an art career, a cool guy life in a hipster NYC neighborhood. Leo left me here to rot, and so I did. I tried my best to pull myself up and start over again, but every time he wriggles back into the picture, I return to this nest of grief I've made for myself. I've wallowed in it for too long, and now I don't even recognize myself anymore. If anyone deserved to be in my position, it was him.

I flip my phone open, punch the number he called from, and press the phone to my ear. It only rings once before I hear his voice again.

"Hey."

"Hey," I say. "Are you busy tonight?"

"I can be free after nine," he says. "Wanna meet up at Shorties?"

I hate Shorties. "Sure."

"Great." I strain to hear Leo's voice. The words are muffled like he's covering the phone and talking to someone else. He uncovers the phone and speaks again, this time in a lower, whispered voice. "I gotta go. I'll see you tonight."

"Bye."

CLICK.

My lips feel thinner as I press them together in a triumphant smile. Meeting Leo is an awful idea. A wonderful, awful idea. The more I let the notion of seeing him marinate, the more my excitement builds. I'm not even upset that I won't look my best for our meeting; in fact, I think it's fitting. He deserves to see me like this. He deserves to be horrified at what I've become.

And he deserves to rot, too.

Chapter Thirteen

Hours pass as I watch golden rays of winter sunlight dance around my bedroom. Bright beams of light crawl along my desk, my television, and my dresser as I sink further and further into bed. I don't get up to eat or pee; I don't need to. Every movement is agony, and whenever I close my eyes, all I see is her face. Those buggy sunglasses and snarling, bloodless lips are forever etched into my mind.

Hours pass, and I'm alive, but don't really want to be. No one else calls to check on me. There is no one who needs me, and I have nowhere that I need to be. The television is my only friend, and I'm even getting sick of that. An infomercial comes on for a product intended to support your breasts while you sleep. Another infomercial for the Ab Circle Pro came on after that, a machine that you use on your hands and knees with your ass in the air, twisting your core side to side to get bodybuilder abs somehow. Now that I can barely move without pain, all of these products designed to make people feel bad about themselves seem even more ridiculous. There was a time before when I didn't care about my looks, didn't care about Leo. A time when I cared about my art and had hope for the future. Things to work toward, plans and dreams. Why did it take losing my toe to realize that I didn't want to lose everything else?

The sound of Elaine coming home breaks the monotony of my lonely day. My heart beats fast, and I mute the TV to listen to the sounds of her talking on the phone. Dust motes hover and swirl in the waning rays of sunlight, and I wonder if they are tiny flakes of my dead skin. Human dander. Elaine heats up a spicy-smelling frozen meal in the microwave, and the scraping of metal against tile tells me she's eating in the kitchen. When was the last time I ate anything? I wasn't hungry anyway.

My lashless eyelid twitches as I ponder taking Elaine as one of my victims again. A voice whispers horrible truths, and I clamp my hands over my ears to block out the voice.

It would be easy enough to take her energy.

She's practically a sitting target.

She wasn't always kind to you after the breakup, was she?

It's true. Everyone, including her, expects you to just get on with life; to pull yourself up by your own bootstraps and pretend not to be devastated and lost.

She's not your friend.

Didn't she almost seem annoyed that you weren't as tough as she was?

That you couldn't just cope and move on?

He's just a man, she said. You'll get over it.

Maybe the voice was right. I put my hopes and dreams into starting a life with Leo, and he threw it all away over some one-night stand. How does someone just get over that?

You could grab a bit of her hair from the bathroom.

Pinch off a strand or two from her hairbrush and swallow it down.

Snap a photo of her while she's napping on the couch or eating her stupid yogurt for breakfast.

You would only borrow her energy for a while, of course, until you found someone else to siphon from.

Maybe then she'll understand how it feels to be trapped inside a prison of her own making.

Whoa, hold up. Where did that stream of nasty thoughts come from? Elaine was my friend. *Is* my friend. She can be kind of a bitch, but she doesn't deserve to live this kind of existence. It's not her fault my life turned out this way. I can't let myself think like that again. It isn't me. Maybe my brain is rotting along with my body. I can lose a toe, but I can't lose my wits. Gotta put a lid on that.

"Elaine?" I call out, my voice low and raspy.

Before I can call out for her again, car keys jingle, our apartment door opens and closes, and she's gone again. It's probably for the best. The further she stays away from me, the better. I wonder if Elaine will be back or if she will stay the night at her girlfriend's place again. I wonder if Leo will come home with me tonight. I don't know if I have the strength to meet up with him at all.

The day has gotten away from me again, and the time on my phone tells me I'm running late. What could Leo possibly want to say to me? Does he want to apologize? Does he feel guilty for what he's done? Or does he still miss me like his drunken middle-of-the-night texts often say? In the past, I would be hopeful that he wanted me back. Now, I'm only curious.

It's late by the time I convince myself to finally get up. The bed sheets cling to my skin like a bandage stuck to an open wound, my shoulders and ass glued to my cotton pajamas from the sticky liquid that seeps through my pores. I don't bother showering and make a half-hearted attempt to style my hair before my date with Leo. My arms are weak, and every time I wind my hair around the curling iron barrel, a handful of dry, dark hair falls out until only baby fine wisps cling to the top of my head. I toy with the idea of covering up my near-baldness with a wig, but then decide to leave it alone. If my ex wants to see me, he'll get the real me. The effect of my scalp showing through in patchy spots was shocking, but I want Leo to experience for himself what's becoming of me.

I have no more eyebrows or eyelashes to speak of, so I draw some brows with a pencil and glue on my last set of false eyelashes. My lips are thin and dry, so I apply a plumping gloss that I stole last summer from Laura Mercier in a hue called Wild Berry. I wear tights and a strappy silver cocktail dress I bought for the last New Year's Eve I spent with Leo in hopes that it sparks a memory. It's still cold and dreary out, so I wrap a silk handkerchief around my head and bundle up in my fur coat. When my going-out look is complete, the mirror shows me a desperate woman. I could be Little Edie Beale's sister.

"This is it," I say to my reflection. "This is the look of the night."

At 8:45, I call a cab to take me to the bar. I barely have enough strength to stand, let alone to drive, but I push past my exhaustion for this one last time. The promise of seeing Leo again and my newfound taste for revenge propel me to move despite my aching joints and weak limbs. Missing a toe didn't make walking easier either, but thankfully, my only pair of flats helped even things out a bit. I wonder what Leo will do when he sees me in this state. I hope he chokes. I hope he screams.

I sit at the foot of my stairs with my sunglasses on, cocooned in my faux fur coat. I rather enjoy the skin-slicing sensation of the wind as it licks against my nose and cheekbones. A few wisps of my remaining hair peek out from under the scarf and blow away in the wind like dandelions. I admire my hands under the parking lot lighting. I'd forgotten to cover up the gash on my knuckles, and I see a flash of white where the bone peeks through. All of my fingernails are gone now, too. Such an odd thing, fingernails. Talons would be much more useful.

The cab driver arrives and smiles at me as I get in. It only takes a moment for her enthusiastic demeanor to change as my musk permeates the cab. She rolls down her windows, asks where I'm going, and offers me a mint. I smile and decline, happy with the notion that I'm filling this woman's taxi with my rancid disease. I want everyone to be uncomfortable with my presence, from the way I look and sound, right down to the way I smell. For so long, I was worried about looking and acting a certain way. Restricting myself to fit into a certain size and styling myself to be visually pleasing for my clients. Now that my body is falling apart, it's almost freeing to be so repugnant. To go from being a thing that men consume to looking like a repulsive monster exhilarated me. If it weren't for the fact that I was losing body parts at an alarming rate, I would happily stay in this horrifying state forever.

My day of rest seems to have given me just enough energy to get ready and leave the house, though perhaps the nagging notion of not wanting to rot away was also responsible for getting me up and out. Honestly, if Leo hadn't called me, I still would be happily nestled between my stinking sheets, allowing my skin to drip off my body and become one with the mattress. Even though I could have targeted Elaine and stolen her energy, deep down, I know I never could. If anyone else deserved to be on the receiving end of this curse, it was my shithead ex. If what the woman said was true, meeting with Leo and performing the steps just as she told me would restore my energy and bring me back to life. I only have to get through this date, and everything will be cleared up and back to normal again.

The taxi driver drops me off at Shorties, and the atmosphere is just as I remember it: dark and smoky and mildly depressing. In the early days of our relationship, Leo and I would use fake IDs to sneak into the bar where I would watch him down cheap beers and play darts, and then after-wards, we would sometimes get into a fight. We share too many memories here, and not all of them are good.

I push my way through the sea of bodies toward the bar where he's already waiting for me, his denim jacket and the back of his head recognizable to me even from a thousand paces. A few days ago, seeing Leo in person would have thrown me into a tailspin. I would have dissolved into a puddle of tears, frozen by my own anguish, disappointment, and grief at the life we were supposed to have together. In this new, destroyed, transformed version of myself, I don't feel any of that. Instead of anxiety, I seethe with vengeance. Instead of yearning, I am consumed with greed. I'm going to get back what he has stolen from me, one way or the other.

Chapter Fourteen

"Hey, stranger," I say, and slide in next to Leo. Up close, he looks fleshier than the last time I saw him, likely from too much stress and craft beer. He turns to face me with a smile that quickly melts away. His long hair is gathered on top of his head in a messy bun, his beard shaggy and sprinkled with a few new flecks of silver. It's been a long time since I saw him in person. How did I not notice how small his eyes are, how perfectly normal and not special at all he is?

He blinks in surprise as I lay my handbag on the counter, stammering at me with beer-scented breath. "Hey. Oh... Oh, wow."

I remove my head scarf, scratch an itchy patch of scalp, and smile. "I see you started without me."

Leo's nose twitches, and his gaze trails up and down my body. "It's...good to see you."

"Good to see you too!" I say oozing as much upbeat enthusiasm as I can stand. "I was hoping you would call me up around Christmas, but you never did."

"No." Leo flinches and leans as far away from me as he can. "So, um. How are things?"

"Great! Really good," I say. "I've been doing some painting. Thinking of maybe getting my collection together to do a gallery showing finally."

"Sounds good." He opens his mouth to speak again and then stammers. "What's, um… What's new?"

"Same old, same old," I say. "How's the baby?"

He squirms at the mention of his child. "Fine. She's getting big."

"Why didn't they come with you?"

Leo shrugs. "Her mom thinks she's too young to travel just yet. Airplane germs and all."

"Right. Well, it's good to see you." I smile and lean closer. He flinches and hunches his shoulders as if bracing for a blow. I had hoped that our meeting would make him uncomfortable, and by all means, my appearance seems to be working just as I had hoped. In the past, Leo had been so unshakable. Unbothered. So fucking cool.

"Leo, why are you here?"

He puts his glass down, belches under his breath, and gives me a long look. "I wanted to see if you were okay."

"That's it?"

"Yeah, I just wanted to check on an old friend…"

"An old friend." I let out a loud, obnoxious laugh. "We were still fucking when you left for Brooklyn. You call me drunk in the middle of the night when your fiancée and baby are asleep, every other month. Doesn't sound like we're just friends to me."

The color in his already flushed face deepens. "Don't be like that."

"Like what?" I smile. "Leo, I don't want to do this anymore."

"Good." He snorts. "I don't need all your crazy bullshit anyway. I'm just here to check up on you and make sure you're okay."

"Oh yeah? Did Elaine put you up to this?"

He sighs. "You're just. You don't look well, baby."

"DON'T YOU DARE CALL ME BABY!"

Spittle froths at the corners of my mouth, and my cool, faux saccharine demeanor slips. The laughter and murmuring voices around us go quiet, the beat of an electronic indie song slicing through the tension between us. I clear my throat, smile, and smooth down my non-existent hair.

"God, not this again." Leo grips his beer glass and stares at the back wall.

Women in peplum dresses and sky-high heels and men in business casual blazers stare at us. They eye me with curiosity. With wonder. With pity and disgust. Time to pull out the stops.

"Leo! What's wrong? What did I do?" I let out a deep, throaty sob and wail.

His shoulders hunch, and he turns back to face me. "Seriously, what the fuck? What have you done to yourself?"

"I haven't done anything!" I cry, louder this time. "I'm fine!"

"It was always something with you, always with the

theatrics." He snorts into his beer, takes a swig, and glances at me. "This is why I left, you know. You're too much."

I shake my head. "No. No, I'm not. You're just a selfish dick."

"Look, I don't know what's up with you, but I've gotta go." Leo gulps down the rest of his beer and signals to the bartender.

"That's it?" I shout at him. "You call me out of the blue, and now you're just gonna bail on me? Again?"

He sighs. "It's not that. Right before you got here, my Mom called. Dad slipped and hit his head. They're headed to the Emergency Room. I need to get down there to be with them."

"Liar." I cough into my open hand, a hacking, wet bark. Red chunks mingle with a slime of mucus on my palm, and I show it to Leo. "Do you have a napkin?"

"Uh." His eyes widen. "Holy shit. Dude, are you sick?"

I wipe my hand on my fur coat. "Don't worry about a napkin, I got it."

"Jesus." Leo presses his lips together, his flushed cheeks puffing as though he were holding back a wave of vomit.

The bartender arrives with Leo's bill. He gives me a pleasant smile, which instantly fades. "What can I get you?"

"Oh, nothing for me," I say. "Thank you."

Leo places forty bucks on the tab and stands up. He wobbles a bit on his feet, and I wonder exactly how many beers he consumed before my arrival. He's trying to escape, but I won't let him.

"I'm sorry, I really wanted us to catch up," he says. "It's just, you know. Gotta go take care of family stuff."

"I understand," I hack up another pink, chunky globule of spit and wipe it on my jacket. "Maybe next time."

"It was good to see you." He is unable to contain his true feelings any longer, his face a portrait of horrified emotion. "Just, um, take care of yourself. Okay?"

"Walk me out?" I ask, batting my false lashes. The glue has worn off on my left lid, and the weight of the unstuck lash is causing my eye to droop like a creepy old baby doll. "I need to call a cab."

"Sure."

Leo walks ahead of me through the crowd, just like he always used to. I follow him out of the cave-like bar into the chilly evening and wonder if he walks ahead of his fiancée. I wonder what his baby looks like. I wonder if my plan will work.

"Listen, my car is over there. I'm sorry to leave things like this, but I really have to go," he says. "Are you going to be alright waiting here for your cab?"

Before he can answer, I pull out my phone. I face the camera toward him and take a photo. His surprised image stares back at me, grainy, but similar enough to the portraits hanging on the woman's penthouse walls. This will do.

"Delete that," he says. "Gretchen is already suspicious. I don't need her getting wind that we met up while I was here."

"Don't worry, baby. I won't tell if you won't."

Like a viper, my hand strikes out and snakes around the back of his neck. He recoils and tries to push me away, but I'm too focused on the task at hand. For months on end, I lived in misery, aching to have him back. I wanted to touch him, to feel safe in his embrace, for things to be the way they used to be.

Every time he called me drunk and lonely in the middle of the night, the invisible tether between us tightened again. So long as I answered his calls and texts, he still strung me along to keep my hope alive and feed his ego. His escape hatch for when life in Brooklyn wasn't working out how he wanted it to. All the while, I was here, lonely and wasting away in a shitty situation I created for myself. He deserves to pay for the way he treated me. He left me here to rot, and so he should rot too. With my last bit of strength, I pull his face to mine, open my mouth, and bite his lower lip.

"Aaaagh!" His gurgled cries are muffled as I clamp down. My teeth feel brittle, but they're still sharp and strong enough to break the skin. His chin hair scratches my face, and I taste iron. Warm liquid coats my tongue, and a synapse in my brain snaps, pops, and fizzles to life. He pushes me away, knocking my phone from my hand, and I fall to the sidewalk laughing. My chin is painted with his blood, a fistful of his hair in the palm of my hands.

"Crazy bitch!" He spits on the ground and wipes his mouth with the back of his sleeve. "I came out here to help you, but you're too far gone! Fucking meth head!"

Leo doesn't help me up or wait around to see what I will do next. He turns and runs away, just like always. Like a coward.

"Make sure to go get that stitched up at the ER," I shout after him, giggling.

I'm giddy, still laughing as I pick my phone up off the sidewalk and rise to my feet. A few drunk patrons hover at the entrance of the bar, craning their necks to get a look at the commotion. Despite the fact that a man has just pushed me to the ground, no one checks to see if I'm okay. The bouncer gives me a disgusted look. I flash my pink teeth at him, hiss, and stalk off in the opposite direction.

My thoughts wander back to the woman again, and that night I saw her behind my apartment. Walking home alone at night used to frighten me, but in this horrifying state, I know that I have nothing to fear. I am the thing in the dark that others run from now. I place the fistful of Leo's hair on my tongue and chew, his image safely stored away on my flip phone. My image now. My life force. Mine.

I don't have to wonder for much longer if the ritual worked. Just like the woman said, the effects are almost immediate. My bones and joints are flexible and no longer ache. I have energy again, and my muscles feel strong and lean and limber. I know it's cold out, but I don't feel anything; the only sensation I register is pure bliss. I pull out my phone to call another cab when I notice something else strange.

I'm not walking anymore, but I'm still moving. It's as though I'm standing on an invisible conveyor belt that pushes me through the air. My feet are inches from the ground, and the sidewalk is speeding under my feet. I'm not just moving. I'm *floating*.

"Fuck yes!" I release a triumphant howl into the night, clutching my phone to my heart as I float all the way home.

Chapter Fifteen

Elaine is asleep on the living room couch when I return to the apartment. An old romantic black and white movie plays on the TV, and an empty bottle of cheap white wine stands on the coffee table. A light buzzing sound emits from her nose, and a dribble of saliva crusts at the corner of her half-open mouth. She must have had a fight with her girlfriend. Elaine only sleeps on the couch when she's upset. I cover her with one of her crochet blankets, turn off the TV, and head for the bathroom.

The shower water is blissfully hot, steaming up our chilly bathroom in an instant. I step in and luxuriate in the sensation of scalding water pouring over my body. I'm no longer tired or in pain; in fact, I've never felt better. I can't remember feeling this comfortable in my own skin, maybe not since I was a little girl. Maybe not ever. Leo's essence has transformed me, just like the woman said it would.

Even though I don't have much hair left, I still pour

shampoo into my palms. I scrub my scalp, and as my fingertips probe the skin on top of my head, something strange happens. The ends of my fingertips are hard and sharp. I glance at my sudsy hands and am surprised to see that my nails have grown back in. Not false acrylic nails; my *real* nails. Strong, pink nail beds with hard, shiny nails and white tips that gleam in the soft bathroom light. I glance down at my feet, hopeful, but I still only have nine toes.

As I suds up my scalp, I sense fresh hair follicles sprouting from the roots. A dandruff commercial comes to mind as I lather, my scalp tingling with the flow of blood, the landscape of my head transforming under a stream of running water. The push of new hair growth erupts through the top of my head in a sensation that's unreal, unlike anything I've ever experienced before. Even through the constant patter of scalding shower head raindrops, I can tell that something is happening. Growing. By the time I'm ready to condition, new strands of dark hair fall thick and lush around my shoulders once more. I run my tongue along my teeth, and they feel strong, sharp, and wonderful, anchored by the root into my skull, which is permanent and immovable.

I use a loofah George got me from the sponge docks to scrub away the stinking dead skin cells on my arms and breasts and belly and legs. Chunks of bloodless, ashen gloop fall into the bathtub like melted wax, revealing smooth, fresh skin beneath. By the time I'm finished with my shower, the tub is clogged up to my ankles. I step out of the bathtub transformed, renewed, more sleek and firm and plump than before. All that's left of my former rotting self is collected now in a soup of soapy flesh water.

I'm back.

The mirror is fogged as I approach the vanity, and I hold my breath. This is the moment of truth. I feel good on the inside, but will I look as good on the outside too? I use the palm of my hand to wipe away the condensation on the mirror and gasp.

I know her. I remember the girl—the woman—who stares back at me. Her hair is long and healthy. Her eyes are clear and lit from within again. Her skin is smooth and free of blemishes, flushed with a rosy hue from within. She no longer smells like a rotting corpse, but of coconut shampoo and Lever 2000 soap. She's missing a toe, but other than that, she's beautiful. Resplendent. Powerful. Unstoppable.

Still nude and dripping wet, I pour drain cleaner into the tub. Instantly, the drain makes a suction sound, and pieces of me swirl down the drain in a tornado of blood and skin. Satisfied with my plumbing job, I exit the bathroom and crawl into bed on top of my covers, grinning like mad. I leave the television off and lie in the dark, listening to the beat of my wicked heart until I slip into a chrysalis sleep.

———

In my dreams, I'm back at the woman's condo again. This time, I know that the condo is mine, that it belongs to me, and that I live there. I know this in the way that we all know things when we dream; that the dreamland experiences are fact, and that in the realm of dreams, rhyme and reason do not exist. In this dream, I am dressed like her in a big, oversized fur coat, and I'm in full control. The woman crouches at my feet, nude and wearing only a dog collar. I laugh at her and peel a strip of skin from my face. She gazes up at me lovingly from the floor, mouth open wide and begging. She barks, and I feed her a strip of my flesh. Then another. Then another. TheN—

Elaine is banging on my door and calling to me. I sit up in bed as my door swings open wide. My roommate stands in the doorway dressed for work. Her gaze locks with mine for a brief moment before she scans me up and down. I forgot that I fell asleep nude.

"Shit! Oh my god, I'm so sorry." Elaine covers her eyes and turns away. "I've been knocking all morning! I had to pick the lock. I thought you were unconscious."

"I was finally getting some good sleep for once." I yawn and stretch. My restored limbs are exquisite. I frown at the foot with only four toes. A small price.

"I was just leaving for work and wanted to check on you. I'm glad you're okay."

I admire my new flawless body. "I'm better than okay."

"Um, there's some mail for you on the kitchen table," she says. "Looks like important stuff."

"I'll look at it later."

"Sorry. I'll leave you alone."

Elaine closes the door, and I lie back on my pillow. A full, restful night of sleep. No more aches and pains. I can hardly believe it. I swing my legs over the edge of the bed and I stand up, weightless, vibrant, free. My stuffed closet door is wide open, and I reach for a charmeuse robe that I stole from Neiman Marcus back when Leo and I were still together. The sensation of silk against my new skin is unbelievably luxurious.

I glance at my desk and remember my unanswered emails

from clients. I need to respond to them soon or they'll move on or forget to pay me, but part of me doesn't want to. The sugar baby/internet model lifestyle was only supposed to be temporary; a fix until I could get back on my feet and return to the art world. I'm afraid that so far, I haven't been very good at being a sugar baby or an artist. At this point, I'd be very happy just to work at a grocery store again.

My phone rests on the closed laptop, and I realize I've let it go dead. I plug it into the wall charger and wait for the screen to light up. There's a voicemail waiting. I press the icon and listen.

"Hey, sweetie, it's Mom. I thought you were going to call this weekend. I hope everything is okay. Call me!"

Shit. I completely forgot that I was supposed to go over there next weekend. I'm glad I didn't end up going to see her in my former state. Not that I had the energy to drive all the way there. I couldn't have let her see me like that, falling apart and smelling like the bottom of a trash can. I'll call her later and make it up to her.

I wander out into the kitchen in search of food, hungry for the first time in days. Thankfully, the fridge and pantry are still stocked with all of the fresh fruits and lean proteins I had purchased the day before. I fix myself a huge salad in a Pyrex mixing bowl and eat the whole thing over the sink.

When I've finished my meal, I glance at the kitchen table. The round basket Elaine and I keep our mail in is full of envelopes addressed to me. Collection notices. Overdue credit card statements. Exciting invitations to apply for a new Platinum Visa! I throw them all away except for one. An official letter from Remington College, sealed in a big, thick envelope.

My pulse ratchets up as I slice the letter open. It had been so long since I applied for the grant and scholarship to Remington that I had given up hope. There was a brief moment right after Leo told me about his new girlfriend and baby, when I tried to pick myself up and applied for some things. I tried to put my head down and keep moving forward like nothing happened, but it didn't last long. During that time, I applied for jobs and scholarships all over the country, but nothing came of it. Now, nearly a year later, a response.

The letter is straightforward and positive. I nearly scream as I glance over the words and read PLEASED TO INFORM YOU, SCHOLARSHIP GRANT, and $100,000. I lost hope on this scholarship so long ago that I didn't even dream I was still in the running. So many more worthy and deserving artists I knew from the gallery days had also applied for this grant. Why out of every applicant did they pick me? My eyes blur with tears as I try to read the rest of the letter. I'm so excited and in disbelief that I nearly pee my pants.

Elated, I head to the bathroom and sit down to urinate for the first time in days. My first choice of art school picked me —*me*—out of thousands of entrants. I didn't think that my portfolio was even that good, but someone must have seen something in my work. This news is the break I've been waiting for. The thing that I needed to help boost me back up and get me back on track.

A horrible aroma hits my nose as I release a stream of urine into the bowl. What comes out of me is not a free-flowing stream of healthy urine but an unspeakable, awful sludge. Thick brown liquid fills the bowl, the color of rusty, discolored water sitting too long in stagnant pipes. My urine smells the way that my skin, breath, and hair used to smell, like rotten death. Perhaps I'm not finished transforming after all. Maybe I just need to drink more water.

I flush the toilet and brush my teeth, still amazed at the creature I've become. Apart from my gross pee, I feel like a new person practically overnight, even better than before I met the strange woman. I drop my robe to the floor, admiring the lift of my breasts and ass and the tight, smooth skin on the back of my thighs where cellulite had once set in. I was perfect. Well, almost. My feet would never be the same. Good thing I was retiring from the fetish and sugar baby game. That's when I remembered.

George.

He still owed me money. Time to pay him a visit.

Chapter Sixteen

I pull into the parking lot of the Wiseman, Keller & Sachs law firm later that morning, more invigorated than I've ever felt in my life. Even though I'm feeling better, I didn't bother to get glammed up the way George usually wanted me to. No blonde wig or heavy makeup. No push-up bra or flirty dress or fake nails. Just the old me in sneakers, faded jeans, and a paint-splattered tee from the GAP. The *real* me was back and more powerful than ever, and I was determined to get my payday.

The law firm is in an old concrete and stucco building adjacent to a dentist and across the street from my favorite grocery store. Shady palm trees and waxy yellow and green bushes line the bland mid-century exterior, offering the only splash of color in the otherwise black and gray parking lot. I've passed this building many times since I was a girl and grew up knowing the law firm's radio jingle by heart.

Wiseman, Keller & Sachs gonna get you the big bucks!

The jingle was followed by the cha-ching of a cash register and the clinking of change. Funny, now that I think of it. I'll be getting big bucks from Wiseman, Keller & Sachs after all, but in a way that I could have never imagined.

I park in a visitor's spot and stride into the office through automatic double doors. The building is tidy and clean, though somewhat in need of a decor upgrade. The faux wood panels and cheap tile don't match the gilded sign on the building or the prestigious air that George liked to pretend surrounded his practice. For the first time, I consider that maybe George isn't as wealthy as he likes to portray himself. Maybe he's cosplaying too.

I sidle up to the front desk with my chin held high, gazing around the office and wondering which office belongs to George as the receptionist takes a call. She's a young woman about my age, slim and deeply bronzed in the way tanning bed addicts are. Her cerulean blue bodycon dress with a plunging neckline looks more suited for cocktail hour than the office, but my guess is that George and his associates don't mind. Her eyelashes are coated with a thick layer of mascara, and she flutters them at me as she ends her call. She could be the sister of my Brittany character.

"Do you have an appointment?" She smiles at me. Her teeth are too white and too big for her mouth.

"Yes. Mr. Wiseman should be expecting me."

"One moment." She taps at her keyboard with long, French manicure acrylics, cocks her head to the side and frowns. "I don't see you on his schedule. Are you sure it's today?"

"It definitely is," I say. "Could you call him?"

"Who should I say is here?"

"Brittany," I say. "Just Brittany."

She places the black desk phone to her ear and punches in a series of numbers. Her neutral gaze flicks to me as the phone rings and she forces a smile. I can hear George answer through the earpiece, clear as day.

"There's a Miss Brittany here to see you," the receptionist says. "She's not on your calendar, but she says you're expecting her."

"Tell her I'm busy with another client," George says. "Get rid of her."

Her smile widens. "I will. Thank you."

The receptionist hangs up, and her expression melts from faux-friendly to dismissive. "Mr. Wiseman is busy with another client right now. I can reschedule your appointment, but he's booked until May."

"That's okay," I say, throwing her my own fake smile. "I'll just find him myself."

I turn and walk down the only hallway in the building. There are half a dozen wooden office doors, each one clearly marked with the names of George's law partners.

"You can't go in there!" The receptionist calls after me, heels clacking against the tile floor. "Security!"

"GEORGE!" I yell as loud as I can. "YOU CAN'T HIDE FROM ME!"

The last door on the left opens, and Daddy George's red face emerges. There's a dollop of mayonnaise on the corner of his mouth and a sprinkle of crumbs on his navy lapel. His eyes are wild with anger, and his cheeks are puffed. He deflates when I meet his glare.

"Brittany." He clears his throat and dusts off his jacket. "I'm sorry, now isn't a good time."

"Caught ya at lunch, huh?" I wipe off the white glob on the side of his mouth with my thumb. His surprised gaze is locked on mine as I stick my finger in my mouth and lick it clean.

The receptionist comes up behind me, panting and breathy. "I'm sorry, Mr. Wiseman, I told her you were busy."

"That's okay, Ashley." George sighs. "I was finished with my lunch anyway."

I throw the receptionist a triumphant smile. "Thanks, Ashley."

She returns the look with a death glare as I follow George into his office.

"Take a seat," he says, closing the door behind me.

George's office smells of vinegar, lunch meat, and after-shave. Two black leather armchairs face a large mahogany desk in the center of his office, and I choose the one closest to him. His white walls are bare with the exception of his law degree from the University of Florida and his Florida State bar certificate. There's a stack of files, a Publix sub sandwich wrapper, and an old framed photo of George and his wife sitting on his desk. The family photo is old, likely from ten years ago, when George had darker hair. His son and daughter are teens in the photo, and Mrs. Wiseman is smiling but looks like she is in pain.

"I suppose you're here for the money," George says, easing into his desk chair. "I have to say, I'm surprised to see you. You look like you're feeling much better."

"Much," I say. "And yes, I'm here to collect."

George steeples his fingers under his chin, grinning. "I didn't know you were a natural brunette."

"There are a lot of things you don't know about me," I say. "I'm not here to chat, though. I'm here to get what I'm owed."

"Is that all I ever meant to you? Money?" George asks. "All of our conversations. Our intimate moments. Didn't they mean anything to you?"

"You were a job," I say. "Nothing more."

"That's a real shame," he says. Something nudges my ankle. "Oooh. Sneakers."

I glance down to see George's bare toes stroking my feet from under his desk. "You know, Brittany, now that you're feeling better, we could still have some fun."

"No," I say. "It's like you said. It wasn't working out. We're through."

"Didn't have that last date though." George groans. The clink of a belt buckle coming undone makes my jaw clench.

"Ew." I frown and wrinkle my nose at him. How can he possibly be aroused after eating a footlong sub? Gross.

"Meet me this weekend." His hand is down his pants now. "I'll double the amount."

"No." I yank my foot back, stand, and pull my phone from my back pocket. I flip it open and point the camera at him like a weapon. "We made an agreement, and you're going to stick to it."

"Or else what?" He says, smiling and stroking himself. "Give me your shoe."

"No!"

Sometimes, whenever George used to please himself in my presence, I would get nauseous. I had to mentally go somewhere else and swallow down the waves of nausea, suck it up and try to be professional. I don't know how other sex workers manage to do it, to dissociate during sex acts they don't really want to participate in, but I know enough about myself now that it isn't for me. I can't blank it out anymore or block my feelings. I don't want to.

"I mean it, George. I'm not on the clock for you anymore," I say. "Pay up or else everyone will know about you."

"Come on, Brittany." He groans again. "One last time."

"My name isn't Brittany."

I mash the camera button. The phone captures his image, hunched over en flagrante, red-faced and still covered in crumbs. His grainy image stares back at me from my phone screen, and a rush of triumph flows through me. I've got him. He's mine.

"Pay me now, and I'll delete this. You'll never see or hear from me again."

George stops stroking himself and stares at me. His forehead beads with sweat, the color in his neck and cheeks deepening in the blink of an eye from deep pink to a reddish purple. His pupils are pinpricks, his irises glazed and funny-looking as his lips quiver. He moans and clutches his chest.

Oh no.

"Oh my god, George!" I slip my phone in my back pocket and go to the side of his desk. "Are you having a heart attack?"

A gurgling sound bubbles from his lips, and he reaches for me. I always worried this might happen. Goddammit, why now? Still, I didn't trust George completely. He could be faking. Or he could be dying. I didn't know which was worse.

"Dammit, George! You can't die now!"

I'm frozen with indecision as his thick, wet tongue flops out of his mouth and tumbles to the floor. I stare at the pink, meaty muscle as it pulses on the carpet. I yelp and jump back, but not far enough. The whites of his eyes are fully visible under his heavy lids and streaked through with red veins. His eyes bulge, pushing out of his skull until they meet their threshold and burst from the sockets like exploded grapes. A smattering of gelatinous eye goo slaps against my jeans as George's body seizes and shakes in his rolling chair.

"George!"

The spasms intensify as he brings his hands to his face. His fingers sink into his generous cheeks all the way to the second knuckle, disappearing into the pliable flesh. I'm frozen as he continues to disintegrate, skin melting and fingers pulling away, mound after mound of gloppy, melting flesh. His hair falls to the ground like needles on a dried-out Christmas tree, and chunks of his scalp peel away to expose a smooth, white skull. His body gushes from every orifice, oozing blood and mucus and all sorts of other viscous bodily fluids, but there's nothing I can do to help him. He's no more than a pile of melted flesh now, liquified matter and exposed skeleton inside a Ralph Lauren suit.

What's left of George's body is still quivering as I open his office door and leave Wiseman, Keller & Sachs for the first and last time.

Chapter Seventeen

Everything is numb as I drive away from George's office. I have no destination in mind, no idea where I'm going or what to do. I just saw my former daddy turn into a pile of bones and quivering goo, and I'm freaking the fuck out.

I must be in shock. This was how it felt when Leo called me that day to tell me about his fiancée. About the baby. Like I know that life won't be the same going forward. That nothing will.

My gas tank light blinks at me, and I pull into a Circle K. My legs feel weak and heavy as I get out of the car and grab the gas nozzle. I don't know how much money is left in my account, but I stick my debit card in the reader and begin to pump anyway. I had been counting on my payout from George. Now he's dead, and I'm still broke.

I pump seven dollars' worth of gas and return the nozzle to the holster. A pinky nail comes loose and falls to the ground, and my breath catches. I can't hold it in anymore and let out a choked sob. I pick up my shed fingernail and wail again, locking eyes with a woman pumping gas across the way from me. She stands there open-mouthed with one hand on the gas nozzle and the other on her shiny new SUV. She's young and fresh-looking, wearing a modest floral dress with long hair and life in her eyes. Her back door is open, and a baby is strapped into a backwards car seat, staring at me, too. The woman flinches, but says nothing.

A burly man gassing up a truck big enough to crush my car stares at us, picking his teeth with a toothpick. He smiles at me, chuckling to himself and shaking his head.

I spit at him and scream.

"What the fuck are you looking at?"

Fluid leaks from my eyes. I wipe the wetness from my face, glance at my hands, and gasp. It isn't tears that leak from my eyes, but something else. Something red. Another fingernail falls to the ground, and I hear my spine snap, crackle, and pop like a bowl of rice cereal with milk. My body is wracked with pain from the top of my scalp to the tips of my toes. I can't believe this is happening again.

I can't stop crying either, and I'm bringing too much unnecessary attention to myself. I need to get out of here. I open my car door, and another fingernail falls away. Panic sets in as I realize that a dead ex-daddy and an empty bank account are the least of my problems. I'm falling apart again, only faster this time, and I don't know why.

The young mother and truck guy are still staring as I give them the finger and peel out of the Circle K. There's only one person who can help me now, and I don't want to see her, but I

have no other choice. I speed toward Bay Vista Condominiums as the wind blows through my hair, taking flossy
strands along with it.

By the time I reach the ninth floor at Bay Vista, I've lost
another nail and half of my hair. My joints ache and crunch
beneath my weight, and I worry that one false step will cause
me to break a bone or worse. I'm deteriorating even more
rapidly than before, and the realization causes my chest to
squeeze in panic. What if I can't stop it this time? What if I
become like George?

The little dog barks behind the door of 901, announcing
my arrival before I can even knock. The woman answers, her
usually stony expression replaced with one of genuine
surprise. Her hair is longer now, full and falling to the small of
her back in loose waves. She wears a black silk wrap dress and
black designer pumps, and her clear skin and violet eyes
sparkle.

"What happened?" she asks, carefully wrapping an arm
around my shoulders. She ushers me inside her dark condo,
embracing me tenderly. I shrug against her motherly affection,
but cannot get away.

"I killed a man," I say. "Or at least, I think I did."

"Tell us everything." The woman leads me to her living
room. The dark curtains are drawn, but candles illuminate the
sitting area and reveal a tea party in process. A Victorian-era
service is laid out on a coffee table surrounded by similarly
dressed, gorgeous women. Large square photo albums sit on
the couches beside each woman, guarded at their sides like a
handbag or a beloved child.

"These are my friends," the woman says. "I was just telling

them about you, actually. Funny you should show up at just the right time."

"My, Lydia, she is a beauty." A woman wearing a turban with deep, brown eyes takes out a pair of handheld spectacles to regard me. "Seems like she needs a little touch up, but altogether, very nice."

"I told you," the woman says. *Lydia.* Why had it never occurred to me to ask her name? Perhaps because I hadn't even considered that she may have one. When we first met, she was nothing like the elegant woman who greeted me at the door. She was more animalistic. Feral. Now she's some well-mannered debutante type, entertaining a room full of fancy ladies in a dark parlor in the middle of the day. If I weren't so desperate for help, I would have run out of the room screaming.

I sink into a purple velvet armchair, suddenly feeling like a specimen on display. Each of the women surrounding me is gorgeous, and despite their varying features, they have that same look in their eyes as the woman who attacked me. I recognize the look now. It's hunger.

"So, you killed a man," Lydia says, pouring the tea. She hands me a cup and saucer and offers up a smile. "Tell us everything."

My hand is shaking as I take a sip of the hot liquid. I can sense the tea going down, but I taste nothing. I pause momentarily and wonder if I should trust ingesting anything this woman gives me.

"I went to visit a former client today—George. He owed me money," I say. "I don't know what happened."

"Well, I see that you took my advice, at least," Lydia says.

"You look fresh—well, fresher than the last time I saw you, anyway."

"I did what you told me. I took a photo of another man last night," I say. "An old boyfriend. I also… I bit his lip. You were right. It worked."

"Of course it did," Lydia says. "Now, back to the story about George."

"Right," I say, my gaze flicking around the room. "I didn't intend to do the same thing to George. I just wanted to intimidate him."

"Why?" A woman with bright red lips and a blonde pixie cut glares at me. She has the soft voice and accent of a southern belle.

"He wasn't going to pay me what he promised, so I threatened to expose him," I say. "He backed out of our deal and was demanding that I spend more time with him. He wouldn't take no for an answer."

"Oh my," Lydia says, bending down at my feet. She picks up a small pink oval and places it on my saucer. "Another fingernail. You poor dear. Hurry, finish your story."

The teacup rattles on the saucer. I can't steady my hands. "And he…he wouldn't pay me or take no for an answer. So I took a photo of him, you know, for collateral. And then he just… I don't know how to explain it. He melted."

"Mmm." Pixie Cut woman nods, her sharp features soften. "I think I know what happened."

"What?"

"Was this man older?" Pixie Cut asks.

"Yes."

"Oh, well, that explains your deterioration," Lydia says.

"I didn't consume anything from him," I say. "Not that day, anyhow."

"Are you sure?" Lydia asks. "Even the smallest amount of biological matter is all it takes."

I take another flavorless sip of tea and think back over the events of the morning. "He had some mayo on the side of his mouth. I licked it."

"Ew," Pixie Cut says.

"What's *mayo*?" A woman with a long braid wearing a bold, patterned caftan asks.

"Really, Regina?" Lydia asks. "It's the salad dressing people put on sandwiches."

"Oh." Regina's shoulders drop, and she sinks back into the couch.

"Well, the mayo is the answer then," Lydia says. "You likely consumed some of his saliva or dead skin cells. It doesn't take much for the transfer of energy to work."

"The process is that touchy?" I ask.

"Oh yes, you have to be very careful," Lydia says. "One time I had one of Clemetine's hairs stuck in my teeth. Poor little lamb, I nearly killed her."

"Clementine?"

Lydia leaned over and scooped up her dog. "Yes, my little angel. Thankfully, I only had one painting of her, which I immediately destroyed of course. I learned from then on to never own images of my loved ones again."

"Thanks for telling me now." I place the teacup on the coffee table and leave behind another fingernail. "So what do I do?"

"Simple. Delete the photo." Lydia strokes my hair. She

pulls her hand away, bringing a big clump of hair with it. "You must destroy every image of him that you own. It won't bring your gentleman friend back, but your beauty will return."

"That's all?"

Lydia nods.

I reach into my back pocket and pull out my phone. I had been bluffing with George before, about having incriminating photos of him. The only photo I have of him is the one on my phone, the one I took in his office, right before he liquified. The women seem to hold their breath, each of them attentive and still as a statue, as I hit delete.

It doesn't take long for the rejuvenation process to take place. Just like when I was in the shower, a surge of euphoria shoots through my body, energizing my limbs. My missing nail beds fill in, keratin binding together and shaping into pink, shining ovals right before my eyes. Fresh hair follicles sprout from my scalp, and the aches and pains in my body disappear. Like magic, I am new again.

"There. Much better," Lydia says. "How do you feel?"

"Fine."

"Wonderful!" Lydia says. "Well, I do hate to be rude, but we need to finish our meeting. I'm having a party tomorrow evening, though. We would love it if you came around."

I glance at the group of macabre women, shark-like smiles played out upon all their lips. They're all like Lydia. All like me. I don't want anything to do with them.

"I'll come if I can."

"Excellent."

I get up from my chair without giving any of the women a farewell or without exchanging pleasantries. I don't feel very warm or pleasant toward them. It was clear that they all followed Lydia's ritual, too, that they were all part of some strange collective. The further I stay away from them, the better.

Lydia leads me to the door with the little dog at her heels, and my thoughts return to my own photo again. What would happen if I found the photo she took of me in the mall parking lot? If it was that easy for me to delete George's photo and reverse the process, couldn't I do the same with my own photo as well? The question was where she kept it, and how easily I could get it back.

"You know, on second thought, maybe I will come to your party."

Lydia opens the door for me and smiles. "Wonderful."

I run a hand through my restored hair. It feels good to be back. But not entirely. "See you tomorrow, then. Thank you for your help."

"Oh, and my dear," Lydia says. "Be sure to wear something nice."

I glance down at my paint and gore-splattered t-shirt and jeans as Lydia closes the door.

Chapter Eighteen

On the way home, I stop at the grocery store and buy a hot, juicy rotisserie chicken. I feast on the bird carcass with my hands, gorging on the oily, salty, protein-rich meat. I slurp down skin, flesh, and sinew, and it's gone before I even reach my apartment, leaving nothing but bone. The process of rejuvenation leaves me famished, and my healthy breakfast salad wore off long ago. I needed to eat. Needed to consume. Energy was what I craved.

Back at my apartment, I park, and my thoughts turn to George again. I'm happy to be back to my restored state, but concerned that his death will trace him back to me somehow. Even though I never gave the receptionist or George's law office my real name, a detective could trace me back to the scene somehow. All they would need is a fingerprint or someone to identify my car. But then, would they be able to pin me for murder? What would a coroner say about a man who melted to death in his office chair?

I also think about George's wife and children. I don't know their situation; maybe they had an open marriage. Maybe she knew about me. Even if she didn't know, his death would still be a shock. His children would be without a father. Is this what will eventually happen to Leo? If I don't continue to rejuvenate myself over and over again, is that what will eventually happen to me?

Chicken grease coats my chin, and I wipe it with the back of my hand as I enter my apartment. I'm already thinking about what I'll eat next: maybe a steak or an entire rasher of bacon or a dozen eggs. Elaine sits at the kitchen table reading and enjoying a slice of key lime pie and a cup of coffee. She blinks and puts down her book as I enter the kitchen with my empty rotisserie chicken bag.

"Hey," she says. "I was hoping I could catch you."

"Hi."

"Is now an okay time to talk?"

I toss the bag in the garbage and sit down at the kitchen table. "Sure."

Elaine leans back in her chair, her gaze flitting up and down. "You seem to be feeling better."

"I am," I say. "What's up?"

"I just want to check in," she says. "I know that you've been having a hard time. I might not have been the best friend and roommate these last few months, but I want to try and make up for that."

"It's okay," I say. "I know I disappointed Leticia when I pulled out of the gallery opening. After everything with Leo, I just couldn't bring myself to do it. I've been pretty flaky lately, but I'm trying to be better."

"It's not just that," Elaine says. "I thought maybe you were on drugs or doing something to harm yourself. I didn't know how to get through to you."

I rest my elbows on the kitchen table. "I'm sorry, too. I know I took advantage of our friendship. I was in a really dark place, but I think I'm climbing out of it now."

"Good." Elaine nods. "I just want to make sure you'll be okay when I move in with Leticia. I want to know that you have a plan."

"I think so," I say. "Remember how I applied for that scholarship and grant to Remington?"

"The fancy art school?"

I nod. "They finally got back to me. I got in."

"That's so great!" Elaine says, smiling at me for the first time in ages. "Oh wow!"

"Yeah, so I guess I just need to fill out the paperwork. I'll have to move to Sarasota, but I think the change of scenery will be good for me."

"It will. It really will." Elaine pushes her plate across the table. "Do you want to finish this for me? I'm stuffed."

My stomach growls as I eye the half-finished dessert. Key lime pie is my favorite. I smile and reach for the plate when I remember George. It only took the smallest dollop of mayo to transfer his biological matter to me. Sharing food with Elaine is a bad idea.

"I already ate," I say. "Thanks, though."

"Hey, do you want to go do something together soon?" Elaine asks. "Go to the beach or thrift store shopping? Like old times?"

My heart squeezes. Elaine is the only real friend I have left, and I've been so awful to her. "Yeah. Yeah, I would like that."

"Okay, cool. Maybe we could go on Wednesday? That's my next day off."

"Definitely," I say.

Elaine stands and throws away the rest of her pie. "I'm heading over to Leticia's in a minute. I know she would still love to host a show for you. She asks about you all the time."

"Really?"

"Yeah." Elaine rinses her plate and puts it in the dishwasher. "And for the record, she thinks Leo is an ass. She's on your side."

"I thought she hated me," I say. "I actually saw him last night."

The words slip out of my mouth faster than I can keep them in. Shit. Well, it's not like a bunch of other people at the bar didn't see us together.

"Babe." Elaine crosses her arms at her chest. "That's a bad idea."

"I know. I needed some closure, though," I say. "After last night, I don't think I'll hear from him again."

"That's good at least," she says. "Okay, well, I've got to go. That's amazing news about Remington, though. Really, congrats."

"Thanks," I say.

Elaine leans in for a hug. I press my lips together tight, close my eyes, and try not to breathe. What if I accidentally inhale her dry skin cells, or what if her hair gets in my mouth? What if I can't ever have an intimate relationship with another person again without worrying about siphoning their life force?

She lets go, grabs her tote bag, and leaves. When Elaine is out the door, I finally exhale and rush to the bathroom. Maybe if I brush my teeth quickly enough, I can remove any biological matter that might have been transferred from her to me. I brush and rinse, then repeat, swishing my mouth with water and trying to keep from swallowing any of my own saliva. The thought of accidentally passing on this curse or whatever this is to Elaine, or anyone else, fills me with a sense of doom.

———

The paperwork for my Remington application states that my scholarship and grant money won't go into effect until the Fall semester, so until then, I still need to figure something out. I scour Craigslist for ads looking for month-to-month tenants, and don't love the available options. I want to be an adult, to take care of myself and not rely on my mother for help. I've been too proud for too long, though. Time to make the call.

"Hey, sweetie!" My mother's voice is clear and steady on the phone. "I was getting worried about you."

"Sorry. I was sick over the weekend," I say. "I could barely get out of bed for a few days."

"Are you alright?"

"Yeah," I say. "Better than alright. I got a letter from Remington. They're giving me a full ride grant and scholarship."

"Oh, sweetie, that's wonderful!" My mom squeals so loud I

have to pull the phone away from my ear. "I told you! You're so talented."

"Thanks, Mom," I say. "I'm really excited. The only problem is that the grant doesn't go into effect until Fall Semester. I'll have to move to Sarasota then, but Elaine is moving in with her girlfriend and…"

"Say no more," my mother says. "Come home and stay with me as long as you need to."

"Really?"

"Yes, of course! You're always welcome back home."

Home. The word brings unexpected tears to my eyes. I had invested so much in the idea of Leo being my home. In making this life for myself, in focusing on my art. When it all crashed and burned, I didn't think I could go back.

"Okay, we can talk about it some more," I say. "I'll probably take you up on it."

"Oh, me and the girls will be so excited!" my mother says, making *pspspsps* sounds. "Won't we, Penelope!"

My heart drops as I remember Clementine the dog and how easily she picked up the virus. If I were worried about Elaine catching this, then my mother and her cadre of cats weren't safe either.

"I've gotta go," I say. "Thanks, Mom."

"You're so welcome, baby," she says. "Love you."

"Love you too."

My laptop dings, begging for my attention. I pull up my email and immediately cringe; I have over a hundred unanswered emails and orders from clients. I wiggle my left foot in my sneakers and consider whether I'll be able to be a foot model again with only nine toes. I take out my notebook and start jotting down orders for photos, $5, $10, and $20 at a time. Until I can figure out what exactly is going on with me and how to reverse whatever Lydia did, I still need to make money.

I work all through the rest of the afternoon and into the evening, filling orders and responding to clients, working as fast and efficiently as I can. I have multiple requests for used lingerie, but no money to buy anything new, and not enough of my own personal items to send off. I could go to the mall and steal more, but the idea leaves a metallic taste on my tongue. I don't want to continue stealing. I need to do better going forward and not engage in risky behavior that could get me in trouble or worse. I cancel the orders I can't fill and close my laptop for the night.

The rush I got from shoplifting was always temporary, always leaving me wanting more. It wasn't like I saved much money by shoplifting anyway; I still ended up with a negative bank account and a closet full of clothes I don't even wear. I couldn't give two fucks about the ethics of stealing from evil corporations, but the thought of getting caught, of jeopardizing my future over something as stupid as underwear, made me reconsider what I was doing with my life. Fall Semester at Remington was my new goal now, something positive to work toward. I had to refocus, get back to the person I was before I let myself get derailed by Leo and all of his bullshit.

The canvas I bought over a week ago still sat in the corner of my room in its shopping bag. For the first time in ages, I feel inspired to create again. I pull out my easel, set up the canvas and my paints, and start thinking of a composition when the front door to my apartment opens. I hear Elaine shuffling through the kitchen, then the sounds of her mattress springs as she flops on her bed.

"Elaine?" I pop my head out into the hallway. "Everything okay?"

"Mmmm," she moans. "I feel like hot garbage."

My pulse spikes. "What do you mean?"

"I feel like I've been hit by a truck," she says. "I think maybe I got your flu or whatever."

I hold my breath until my head begins to pound. How could this be possible? I didn't eat her slice of pie, didn't breathe or open my mouth or even blink when she went in for a hug. How could I have infected her?

My face is heating up. I need to think. I splash my face with cold water in the bathroom sink, and that's when I see it. Pink cap. Purple toothbrush. I had been meaning to get a different toothbrush cap for a while. Even though Elaine and I kept our toothbrushes on opposite sides of the sink, the identical caps covering the brushes sometimes caused me to pick up the wrong one.

Pink cap, purple toothbrush. The bristles were still damp. Elaine's toothbrush. The toothbrush I had used only a few hours earlier.

Chapter Nineteen

Elaine and I have been friends since I started college nearly four years earlier. Like me, she was cynical and reserved, but far more responsible and less impulsive than I am. She worked in the pharmacy at the grocery store where I worked as a cashier, her just finishing up pharmacy school, and me just beginning my undergrad studies. We would often take lunch breaks together, bonding over our shared love of art, film, and music, as well as our hatred of the misogynistic store manager. We became fast friends, going to see our favorite indie bands at dive bars, picking out thrift store finds for our apartment, and visiting farmers' markets on the weekend. So many years. So many memories. So many photos.

I needed to destroy them all.

I start with the few photos I had of her on my phone, one where she dumped an entire pot of spaghetti on the floor, and another of her and Leticia at a bar. Then I move on to my computer, scanning thousands of digital photos I downloaded onto a hard drive. Delete, delete, delete. After I clear out my photo folder on my computer, I go through the box of printed photos under my bed and collect every photo of Elaine that I can find, rip them to shreds, and light the pieces on fire in a metal bowl by the dumpster.

When I'm satisfied with my work, I wash my hands and peek in on Elaine. She lies face down on top of her covers, breathing heavily. I want to know for sure that I undid the spell, that she was safe, but I also don't want to disturb her. That's when I smell it: the funky cheese, dirty laundry smell of damp and decay. She rolls over and whimpers, and I can hear the bones in her spine crack as she stretches. She must still be infected. I probably missed a photo somewhere. Are there still photos of her on my Myspace page? In my email? What if I never find them all?

Of all the ways to fuck up, of the people to hurt, I couldn't let it be Elaine. She was too good, too innocent. The world needs more people like her than like me. I deserved to rot and waste away in my own misery, but Elaine? She always worked hard. She was a good person! If I can't figure out how to disinfect her, then I'll never forgive myself. It could take me days or weeks to hunt down every last image of my best friend that I've ever taken, and by then, she could be a pile of bones and goo. There's only one solution to this problem that I can think of. I have to cut this virus off at the source.

I need to get my photo back from Lydia.

I work all through the night deleting files, ripping my closet apart, and flipping through my books and drawers for photos of Elaine. I only stopped to chug water and eat, and eat I most certainly did. I don't know if I'm making up for the last week of sickness and starvation, but throughout the course of the night, I clean out nearly all of the groceries I bought. Three big salads. An entire pint of yogurt. Deli meat. Sliced cheese. Fruit. I gorge and gorge on healthy food, yet still never feel full.

Elaine is still in bed when the first rays of morning sun poke through the blinds. I've been up all night searching, organizing, destroying, cleaning, and I'm not even a bit tired. In fact, I feel even better than before, more energized than after my ill-fated date with Leo. Her energy must still be flowing through me. She doesn't even stir when there's a knock on our apartment door.

I peer out the peephole on my kitchen door and see a woman of about thirty with a short, dark bob of hair wearing a navy business suit. She's accompanied by a clean cut young man wearing designer sunglasses, a dress shirt with no tie, and a shit eating grin. I leave the security chain on and open the door.

"Yes?"

"Hi there, we're looking for someone named Brittany?"

My heart races as I do my best to keep my composure. "I'm sorry, I don't know anyone named Brittany."

"Ma'am, are you sure?" the man asks. He removes his sunglasses and wipes the shitty look from his face. His eyes soften as he smiles at me.

"Yes. What's the problem?"

"We're Detectives O'Grady and Mendez," the woman

explains. "We're investigating the death of a man. Do you know anyone named George Wiseman?"

I shake my head. "No."

"His secretary made a report of a young woman fleeing the scene," the man says. "Said her name was Brittany, early twenties. Matches your description. Is that your Toyota parked near the dumpster?"

I shake my head. "No. I'm sorry, I still don't know what this is about."

"Probably nothing," the woman says, holding up a business card. "Can I give you this?"

"Sure." I take the business card, my hand trembling.

"Were you in the vicinity of the Wiseman, Keller & Sachs law firm yesterday?" the man asks. I can't be sure, but I think he's looking down my shirt.

"I don't know, maybe," I say.

"Where were you yesterday morning?" the woman asks.

"I went to Publix yesterday around noon and picked up a rotisserie chicken. That's about it, though. I've been here since then."

O'Grady and Mendez exchange a look. The man jots something down in a notebook.

I give them my most innocent, sugar baby eyes. "Did I do something wrong?"

"Not at all. Please call us if you think of anything," the woman says. "We may follow up with you, but I think this is all we need for now."

"I still don't know what this is about," I say. "You said a man died? Was it a murder?"

"The circumstances are rather *mysterious*," the man says,

throwing me a flirty smile. He leans in, his voice a whisper. "Between us, the coroner thinks it might be spontaneous combu—"

"Mendez!" The woman smacks the other detective with the back of her hand. "Sorry, ma'am. We're not at liberty to say. Thank you for your time. We'll be on our way now. Again, please don't hesitate to call if you think of anything."

"I will," I say.

Mendez winks at me and returns his sunglasses before following O'Grady down the stairs.

I close the door, lock the deadbolt, and watch the detectives leave through my kitchen blinds, my heart a ticking bomb. *Fuck.* Fucking Ashley! That was way too close. Did George have cameras in his office? I didn't remember seeing any. Without video or photographic evidence, it would be her word against mine. From the looks on the detective's faces, I couldn't tell if I was in the clear, but Mendez's reaction was reassuring. Spontaneous combustion. Why did the detective give me that information so freely?

Power, wealth, beauty, influence. It will all be yours.

Influence. No wonder Lydia had been able to get away with siphoning the life force of young women for so long. If you can talk your way out of trouble, you can literally get away with murder. Beauty, luck, influence, and...floating power? The benefits of this strange new virus are intoxicating, no doubt. The price is too high, though. As I ponder my newly acquired superhuman abilities, I hear my cell phone ring. I let the call go to voicemail, my pulse still hammering away at my veins as I listen to the message.

"Hi, this is Leo's mom, Cindy. I know it's been a while since we last

spoke, but I was wondering if you could call me, please?" Cindy sobs and sniffles. *"An ambulance just came to pick Leo up. He's unresponsive. I know he was with you last night. He was drinking heavily after he came home, and, oh, I just wanted to know if you think he took anything, any drugs or anything? I'm so sorry to bother you. Please, just call us if you can think of anything."*

CLICK.

Cindy had always been so kind to me. I sit on my bed and stare at my phone for a long time. In my desire for revenge and renewal, I pushed away the fact that I wouldn't be hurting just one person, but multiple people. Revenge isn't one and done; it's a butterfly effect of grief that can trickle down generations. What have I done?

I'm fairly certain that I only have one photo left of Leo. When we broke up, I did a thorough, scorched-earth disposal of any photos I had of him, and then I double-checked at my mother's house after his baby was born for any leftover evidence of our time together. Even though I hate Leo, his loved ones don't deserve this pain. His daughter doesn't deserve to go through life without a dad.

I open up my phone, find the photo of Leo, and hit delete.

In the other room, Elaine moans.

Nothing changes for me. I still feel amazing. Powerful. I assume that I'll feel that way until Elaine begins to rot away like George did, only since she's young and healthy, her process will be slower and more painful. After she wastes away, I'll just have to find someone else to prey on, again and again and again, until the end of time. Maybe Lydia could live this way, free from the guilt of harming others, but I couldn't. It was easy enough to harm myself, but not so easy to know that my actions hurt someone else.

I have a new goal now, one that doesn't have anything to do with money or revenge or status. I'm going to make Lydia pay. I'm going to stop her. Only, I don't know how.

Chapter Twenty

E laine is dying. Or at least, it seems like she is.

Around noon, Elaine finally gets out of bed and shuffles to the bathroom. From the hallway, I can hear her crying and puking. I don't think I've ever heard Elaine cry before. My phone rings as Elaine continues to hurl. I pull my phone from my back pocket to see my mother's phone number on the screen. I flip open the phone and press it to my ear.

"Hey, Mom."

"Finally! Oh, sweetie, I've been so worried," my mother says. "Cindy called me. She said Leo is in the hospital?"

"Oh." I sit on the edge of my bed. My mother and Cindy became friends when Leo and I first got together. The fact that their friendship endured long after Leo and I broke up was a hard pill for me to swallow. "Yeah, I got her voicemail. I meant to call her back."

"He was unconscious when they brought him in. I guess he's stable now, but the doctors don't know what happened."

"So weird," I say.

"Cindy says you were with him the other night."

I roll my eyes and bring the phone to my chest. I hear my mother calling my name through the earpiece, but I don't know what to say. I take a breath and put the phone back to my ear.

"Yeah, I saw him."

"Why on earth would you do that?" she asked, her voice tinged with disapproval.

"I needed some closure. I wanted to talk through some things. He asked me out for drinks, and I met him."

"But you don't drink." She sighs. "You know it isn't healthy for you to see him."

"I know. I feel like I got the closure I needed, though. Trust me, I won't be seeing him again."

"Well, that's good at least. Cindy thinks maybe he took some drugs, but the toxicology report came back clean. At first, she was accusing you of giving him something, but I told her you would never do something like that."

I swallow, clutching the phone in my hand tightly. "No. Of course not."

"I'm probably going to go down there to visit. Cindy is so upset. I can come by the apartment while I'm in town. Maybe we can go get dinner."

"No!" I wince. "I mean, Elaine has some kind of stomach bug and she's contagious. Probably caught it from me. I don't want you to get sick either. Just, um, give Cindy my best and I'll catch up with you later, okay?"

"Well, all right." Mom sighs in the way that means she's annoyed. "I love you."

"Love you, too."

We hang up, and before I can think of what to do next, a large thud comes from the bathroom.

"Elaine!"

The bathroom door is locked. I bang on it and rattle the doorknob. She isn't answering, and with every moment that passes, my panic intensifies.

"Elaine! Are you okay?"

Nothing. The door is made of cheap particleboard, and I know it won't take much to get through it. I curl my hand into a fist, punch a hole into the door and unlock the knob from the outside.

I open the bathroom door and find Elaine naked, sprawled halfway on the floor and half-draped over the tub. The shower rod came down with her when she fell, the curtain bunched beneath her, collecting water from the showerhead. Elaine was always pale, but in her sickly, wet state, she looks almost gray. Like a fish plucked from some deep, cold lake. She moans as I turn off the water, wrap her in a towel, and help her up.

"What happened?" she asks. Even though I can tell she tried to wash her body and hair, the scent of decay still hangs heavy on her skin, thick and greasy like an oil slick.

"You fell," I say. "You need to get back in bed."

"I feel like I've been run over," Elaine says. "Is this how it felt when you were sick?"

Guilt stabs me in the chest. "Yeah. Yeah, it was pretty bad."

"I need to call into work," she says, her voice raspy. I gag at the foul odor coming from her mouth. "I don't wanna get in trouble."

"I'll get your phone."

I help Elaine into her bed, alarmed at how rapidly she's deteriorating. Her hair seems thinner and flat, and her arms feel devoid of any muscle tone, soft and flabby beneath my grip. And then, there's the tell-tale smell. The aroma of decay is so offensive that I can barely stand to breathe. Did I look and smell this bad before my rejuvenation process? A quick evaluation shows that Elaine still has all of her fingernails, ears, and toes for now. I know if I don't do something soon, she'll start to fall apart just like I did, one digit at a time. I pull her phone off the charger to see a half dozen missed calls from her girlfriend.

"Leticia has been trying to call you," I say. "Here."

"Thanks." Elaine coughs. "I know she's going to want to come over and take care of me. I don't want her to get sick either."

"Yeah, maybe tell her to stay away." I wince.

Leticia won't stay away. She'll come over to take care of Elaine, and this thing will spread from her to Leticia and then to who knows who else. I'm literally a walking plague, and anyone I know and love isn't safe. I have to end this.

"I'm going to go out in a little while. Do you need anything before I go?"

Elaine shakes her head. "No. I just want to sleep."

"Good idea," I say. "I'll check on you before I leave."

I close Elaine's bedroom door and head to the bathroom to tidy up. The shower curtain is still askew, so I fix it back to the wall and wipe the water from the floor, then head to the kitchen to find something to eat. There isn't much left after my last gorge. My feet don't touch the floor as I consume an entire bag of carrots and three of Elaine's yogurts in front of the open fridge. I make a mental note to replace her yogurt, aching for more protein, more fat, more sugar. I'm still hungry, but there's nothing left to eat in the fridge, and besides, it's getting late.

Wear something nice.

My toes drag along the tile floor as I float to my closet. I don't even have to think about it now, floating is as second nature to me as breathing. I would be lying if I said that I didn't enjoy living in this new, enhanced body where nothing hurts and everything is going my way. I could be successful again at my art. I would never have money problems, never have to entertain a man again if I didn't want to. Any success I have from here on out would be tainted, though, if it comes at the expense of another. I can live with achy knees and a negative bank account, but I can't live with guilt.

My closet is bursting with expensive cocktail dresses, and I wonder why the hell I ever thought they would transform me into someone I never really wanted to be. I tried so hard to reinvent myself as a sexy vixen after Leo left, but my new persona never felt genuine. Underneath the wig and the makeup and the fake nails, I was still me.

I reach for a red spaghetti strap gown I stole from Saks and slip it over my head. Like so many other items in my closet, this one still had the tags attached. The gluttony of stolen, hoarded items on my racks and in my drawers makes me sick. When I get back to normal—*if* I get back to normal—I'm going to give it all away. I'll donate my fanciest dresses to a prom dress drive and stick the rest in the donation bins at the hospice thrift store. My wardrobe and accessories used to mean something to me; symbols of a lifestyle I thought I wanted to lead. Now I can hardly stand to look at any of it.

I've never felt physically better or more powerful, and I've never looked better either. But what good is wealth and influence and success if I can't ever hug my own mother, or kiss someone I love without worrying about accidentally snatching their soul? Going to the party is the only way for me to get answers and end this…whatever this is. George. Leo. Elaine. No one I care about is safe around me, and the longer I live in this enhanced version of myself, the harder it will be to let it go.

Lydia's party is sure to be full of soul-snatching hags, and I don't know what to expect from them. Hanging out with them is not my idea of a good time, but I have to go and pull on a fake smile anyway. Tonight I'm going to make things right. I'm going to search Lydia's condo and get my photo and my life back. But first, that bitch is gonna pay.

Chapter Twenty-One

The ninth floor of Bay Vista is bustling when I arrive later that night. A beautiful man in an expensive-looking tuxedo guards the front door like a sentinel, stony-faced and built like a brick wall. His skin and hair are flawless, but there's no light behind his eyes; a mannequin bouncer for ghouls. Classical music and the murmuring of gossip and exchanges of information spill into the hallway. He takes my coat and offers to take my bag, but I decline.

"Lydia insists," he says, reaching for my bag.

"Hey, hands off!" I swat at his giant mitts. "Why can't I hold on to my bag?"

"No personal items allowed."

"Oh." I frown as another guest pushes past me. This is going to complicate things if I need to sneak out of the party undetected. While he isn't looking, I slip my phone into the top of my strapless bra. I could live without my coat and purse, but my phone is a life preserver I can't be without.

When I have his attention again, I hand him my purse and coat and watch as he secures them in an entryway closet next to all of the other guests' personal items. It's too late to turn back now.

I take a deep breath and head into the viper pit.

Lydia's home is dark, as always, but warmly lit thanks to dozens and dozens of candles. I can't help but wonder if she lit them all herself or had her tuxedoed Igor man servant do it for her. Every surface is aglow, casting flickering incandescent light upon the faces of her guests. Women stand around chatting or lounging on the couch with plates and cups, laughing, talking, drinking, eating. Everyone is gorgeous, flawless, and impeccably dressed in deep colors and rich, textured fabrics. My slinky red dress seems out of place in contrast, a bright spot in a sea of shadows.

Another expressionless, beautiful man in a suit walks by with a tray laden with champagne coupes. He extends the tray toward me, and I take a glass filled with bubbly pink liquid, but do not drink. After my ill-fated brush with margaritas, I know for certain that I don't have a taste for alcohol, and besides, I don't want to trust eating or drinking anything Lydia offers anymore.

A flash of white catches my eye in the distance, and I'm overcome with the feeling of being watched. I recognize Pixie Cut from across the room, and she waves to me, her expression lit up. She links arms with an insanely gorgeous woman who could be Salma Hayek's sister, and the duo makes a beeline for me. I take a deep breath, smile, smile, smile, and get ready to act.

"You made it!" Pixie Cut gushes and leans in. She pecks

me on both cheeks, European style. "Mariel, this is the one we've been telling you about."

"Pleasure to meet you." Mariel extends a hand and offers a limp greeting, then gives Pixie Cut a side eye. "Grey is always enthusiastic when we have a new addition."

"Is that what I am?" I giggle, putting on my best coquette. "Is this some kind of club?"

"More like a lifestyle. It isn't for everyone, babe, but you'll get used to it." Grey nods. "You know, Lydia never told us your name."

"Brittany," I say, shifting into sugar baby mode. Pretend to be someone else. Mask your disgust. Make them happy. "I don't know what to think about all this, actually. I feel great, but I don't know how it all works."

"It's a lot of work, but look at what you can have." Grey waves her arms around. "You know this isn't even Lydia's only penthouse condo. She's got luxury homes all over the world."

Mariel elbows her. "Seriously? You don't need to advertise that."

"This place is nice and all," I say. "I don't necessarily need all of this, though."

"It isn't about need," Mariel says. "It's about want."

"Oh," I say. "Well, I don't know that I really want it then either?"

"So what's the deal then?" Grey's eyes narrow. "You've seen what the rejuvenation process will do. There's no plastic surgeon or nutritionist in the world who can give you these results."

"I guess I just feel bad about what happened," I say. "I didn't mean to hurt my da—George."

"You know, I accidentally melted my first husband," Mariel says, rolling her eyes. "I told him I didn't want to go down on him, but he didn't listen. It was his own fucking fault."

I gag a little, then laugh. "Sounds like maybe he deserved it."

"They all do." Mariel takes a sip of her champagne.

"I don't know if that's true," I say. "How do I keep from hurting people? Like, the people I care about?"

"It's tricky, but you'll learn in time," Grey says. "Until my poor mama died, I wore a face mask around her and wore gloves. Ugh, it was a pain in the butt. You learn to figure it out."

The classical music goes silent, and the metallic *TWONG* of a singing bowl fills the air. The guests cease chattering and turn in unison toward the hypnotic sound. A figure dressed in a sheer black veil and lace mourning gown travels down the hall with another small veiled figure at her side. As they step into the dim light, I can see that the veiled figure is Lydia, and the smaller figure at her side is a child, a girl who couldn't be more than ten.

"Hello, sisters!" Lydia says. "Thank you so much for coming tonight. I know many of you have traveled from afar to be here."

"Hail! Hail!" The women say in unison, raising their champagne coupes.

"Tonight we welcome our newest member in our yearly exchange of souls," Lydia says. "This exchange binds us all and makes us stronger. United. When we share our life energy as a collective, none of us shall ever starve."

I turn to Grey and whisper. "Who's the little girl?"

"Her daughter, shh!" Grey waves me off.

Lydia and the little girl raise their veils. Even in the low light, I can tell that Lydia's energy is drained. Her eyes are sunken, and her skin looks sallow, just like the first night we met. The little girl standing next to her is a carbon copy of her mother, though devoid of the bright eyes and full cheeks a girl her age should have.

"Tonight we witness the dawn of a new era of transformation," Lydia continues, wrapping her arm around the little girl. "It's been a long road, but finally, my daughter will truly be one of us."

"Hail! Hail!"

"The exchange of energy will also seal our newest member as a devotee, as one of us," Lydia raises a champagne coupe in my direction. "You'll have our love and sisterhood and protection for as long as the energy flows."

"Hail. Hail! Let the energy flow!"

My shoulders jump every time her guests repeat the enthusiastic chant. The atmosphere thins, and my ears ring. All of my internal warning systems are flashing on high alert. Suddenly, the pieces fall into place, and I realize what I've walked into. This isn't a party. It's a witchy sorority hazing.

"Sisters, you may begin the exchange however you wish," Lydia says. "Hail! Hail!"

"Hail! Hail!"

I turn to Grey to ask what Lydia means, but she's already busy swapping spit with Mariel. I blink and glance around the room, frozen as I witness a buffet of hedonistic acts playing out before my eyes. The woman in the turban from the other day has opened up a vein in her wrist and is feeding droplets of blood to a pale, slim woman with jet black hair and Bettie Page bangs. Two other women take sips of champagne, clink their glasses, and then exchange cups. All around the room, women are making out, sharing drinks, licking bloody wrists, chewing on hair. There's even a couple propped up on the kitchen island with their skirts hiked over their hips, enthusiastically swapping bodily fluids.

Mariel pulls away from Grey and turns to me. She takes my hand, smiling. "You're turn, love. Pick your pleasure."

"Oh," I say, clearing my throat. "Um, no thanks. I think I'm going to sit this one out."

"But you have to." Grey plucks a white blonde hair from the top of her head. "It's okay. You don't have to do any of the sex stuff. Hair is easy for beginners."

"I just don't think I'm ready," I say. "I don't think all of this is for me."

"Don't be ungrateful." Lydia appears out of nowhere, her black lace skirt rustling as she floats to my side. Her creepy little daughter is at her heels, mirroring her mother's every action like a trained mime. The girl growls and stares up at me hungrily with big, milky eyes and dry, paper bag skin. I've never seen a child look so old.

"I'm sorry, Lydia. I didn't know the party would be like this," I say. "I don't think that I can join in."

"You don't have a choice." Lydia reaches down and plucks a hair from her daughter's head. "This is a necessary part of our cycle. It cannot be broken. You must join in or be destroyed."

"Destroyed?" I laugh. "No thanks. I think I'd better go."

Strong fingers wrap around my upper arms. Grey and Mariel are on either side of my body, their grip firm as they hold me in place.

I start to panic. "Hey! Hands off!"

"Sorry, sweetie," Grey says. "Lydia's right, though. It's for the best."

I try to wrench my arms out of their grasp, but they're stronger than I am. Lydia advances toward me and I kick my feet out from under myself and drop my ass to the floor like a child throwing a temper tantrum. Grey and Mariel struggle to keep hold of me as Lydia extends a single strand of hair from her weird little old lady kid toward my face.

"No!"

I bring my knee to my chest and deliver a swift high-heeled kick to Lydia's solar plexus. My eyes go wide as her face contorts into a gaping, black-eyed scream. My kick sends her sailing backward as though she were light as air, a piñata filled with sawdust and despair.

Grey and Mariel drop me to attend to their mistress, and I scramble back. Women descend upon me from every angle, hissing and clawing at my back with dagger-like fingernails that rake my exposed flesh. Another woman pulls my hair, the strands popping and tearing away from my scalp, but I keep moving. The guard at the door is nowhere to be found, and I take the opportunity to run. I don't bother looking for my coat or my purse. I don't bother taking the elevator.

Instead, I run straight through a glass window and sail into the cool, dark night.

Chapter Twenty-Two

Flying is really fucking weird. The movies would have you think that it's easy, that you just spread out your arms and soar like Superman, but it's not. I didn't know that I could fly when I launched out of the ninth-floor window of Bay Vista Condominiums. I only hoped maybe I could float down to the ground or something. But it turns out that I *can* fly, just not very well.

A chilly breeze kicks off the gulf as I hover above the beach, the sandy shoreline nearly a hundred feet below me. Every time I try to right myself, a gust of wind knocks me for a loop and sends me tumbling through the air. I don't have a plan, don't know where I am going; I only know that I need to get away from those hags. I don't want to take part in their fucked up rituals. I don't want to support their way of life or be tied to them in any way.

After a minute, I give up trying to fly and ease down to earth, my bare feet landing in the sand. Somewhere along the way, I had lost my shoes, and without my coat or my purse, I am both freezing and stranded. Thankfully, I'm still in one piece after crashing through a double-paned window, with not a scratch on me. I need to find a way home, but calling a cab is the least of my worries.

I am being followed.

"Where you going, baby girl?" Grey cackles, hovering above me. "The party is back there!"

"Fuck off!" I kick a spray of sugar sand up in the air. A healthy dose hits her between the eyes.

Grey screeches and claws at her face. "Mariel! Get her!"

My scalp burns as I'm pulled up and away from the beach by my hair. Mariel cackles, her fetid breath as hot and horrible in my ear as a July breeze kicking off a red tide bay.

"You think you're special, don't you?" Mariel hisses. "You're just fodder! You're nothing!"

"Let me go!" I shout, kicking my feet in the air. "Bitch!"

"I know your type." Mariel cackles. "Always think they're too good to hurt another person. Face it, darling, none of us are innocent. Everyone who has ever breathed a breath of life is here to consume. To kill. To take. You are no saint."

"Well, I'm sure as hell not like you!"

I levitate just enough to ease the tension on my scalp and meet Mariel eye to eye. The sneer falls from her lips as I sink my nails into her hand and rip the flesh away.

"No!"

She releases her grip on me and brings her injured hand to her chest. Grey has hold of my foot, and I deliver a kick to her face with my free leg. I gasp as the lower half of her goes sailing into the night and lands on the foamy shoreline with a plunk.

I smile and let out a cackle of my own. I'm stronger than they are! No wonder Lydia and her fucked up knitting circle all wanted a piece of me. I try my hand at flying again, this time steadier in the air than before. I leave the injured bitches moaning on the beach and float up, up, up, through the night toward home.

———

Okay, so maybe flying is growing on me.

Once I figured out how to position my body and use the wind currents, it wasn't too bad. And at night, my little town by the bay is actually quite pretty. I worry that Lydia might send more of her goons after me, so I hang out and watch the Bay Vistas building for a while, crouching on the roof of a nearby Holiday Inn like some kind of fucked up gargoyle. I discover a group of nesting seagulls on the roof, and they look at me as though I don't belong there. They're right, I don't. But there I am, and there I stay until it's nearly dawn.

I watch the exit to the condo building all night, waiting for another attack, but nothing comes. As dawn nears, it occurs to me that they likely won't go outside during the daytime if they can help it. I only saw Lydia outside during the early morning hours and in the evening, and even then, she always seemed to need to shield herself from the light. Is she a vampire? A witch? Whatever the fuck she is, I know that I am well on my way to becoming like her. And if I don't want to stay this way, I need to try something. But I won't have much time.

When the sky begins to turn a shade of lavender and then pink, I finally decide it is safe to go home. I float down from the hotel rooftop and find my way to the main road, floating quickly through side streets. In the early dawn light, if someone were to see me on the side of the road, they would see a strange woman in a red evening gown, seemingly riding a bike. If they look close enough, they would see the truth: that there is nothing between me and the sidewalk but air.

I arrive home just before the street lights go out and dawn arrives in full form. I am locked out and don't have my house keys; Igor had made certain of that. I could knock on our apartment door, but I also don't know how deeply asleep Elaine is. There is only one sensible solution. I have to tap on her window.

I float around the side of my apartment building, stunned at how shoddy the exterior siding looks. Half of it seems to have rotted away or been eaten by termites, though I have never noticed before, probably because I have never had cause or ability to float around this side of my apartment building. When I reach Elaine's window, I glance around, hoping that she'll answer right away. If I float out here in the open for too long, where all of my neighbors can see, eventually, I'll be spotted.

KNOCK.

KNOCK.

KNOCK.

I rap silently against the glass, then louder and faster.

Finally, her pink curtains rustle, and Elaine's pallid, exhausted face comes into view.

"What are you doing out there?" she asks.

"I need you to let me in," I say. "I lost my keys and my phone. My wallet. Everything. Please, Elaine, I don't want to wait out here."

She glances down at the street, then back up at my face. Her drooping, sleep-deprived eyelids widen, and her lips form an "O" of surprise. "What's going on?"

"I'm locked out!" I shout. "Come on, I need you to let me in before someone sees me."

"How are you doing that?" She glances up, down, and all around. "Are you on a wire or something?"

"No! Come on, I'll explain later."

"Wait, are you a vampire?"

"No!" I shout, glancing over my shoulder. "Maybe? Fuck, I don't know. Please, Elaine. Just let me in!"

"Really? Because I've seen Lost Boys and you sure look like a fucking vampire."

I show her my teeth. "Look! See? No fangs! Come on, I promise, I'm not a vampire.

"That's totally something a vampire would say!" Elaine coughs into her open hand. Through the pane of glass, I can see specks of red on her palm. She's getting worse.

"Elaine, you're sick and it's all my fault. But if you let me in, I can fix this. I can make you better again."

"What do you mean?" Elaine asks.

I hear my neighbor's door open below. People are waking up. I need to move.

"I'll explain it, just come on! Open the window!" I say. "I'd break the glass and come in, but we don't want to lose our deposit, right?"

"Fine." Elaine sighs. She unlocks the window and tries to push it open. I can hear her grunting on the other side, straining. She's out of energy.

"I got it," I say, and pull off the screen. The window lifts without a problem for me. I pull myself into Elaine's room and am immediately hit with that funky rot smell. I keep her window open to let the room air out.

"Thanks," I say. "I know this is weird."

"Really fucking weird," Elaine says. "What's going on?"

"I think some kind of energy soul sucking coven infected me," I say. "Then, I accidentally infected you."

"What? That's ridiculous." Elaine coughs. There's more red-tinged spittle on her hand. She's deteriorating fast. "How could that even happen?"

"I used your toothbrush by accident," I say. "This virus that I have is spread through sharing biological matter. Sorry."

"I told you that would happen," she says, sputtering into another bloody coughing fit. "I think…I think maybe I should just go to the emergency room. I'm clearly hallucinating."

My gaze flicks to Elaine's dresser. There's a photo of her and Leticia kissing from her birthday last year tucked into the frame of the mirror. A photo that I took.

"Oh my gosh. Elaine! That's it!"

I snatch the photo from her dresser mirror and tear it in half. I rip the pieces of the photo over and over again until the image is nothing but confetti.

"Hey! What's your problem?" Elaine cries. "I thought you liked Leticia? That's my favorite picture of us."

"Yeah, it's a photo I took," I say. "See, however this fucked up coven works, they steal your essence through images and organic body matter or some shit."

"Coven? You mean like witches? Do you hear yourself?"

"I know! It sounds nuts, but you just saw me floating, right? I don't know *what* they are, and I don't care. I just want them to leave me alone."

"This is too much," Elaine says. "I'm going to call Leticia and have her take me to the hospital now."

"No! Just hold on for a second," I say. "If this is truly the last remaining photo I took of you, then ripping it up should break the spell."

"What do you mean by spell? None of this makes sense." Elaine's head cocks to the side. She sticks her finger in her right ear and twists it around. "Did you hear that?"

"Hear what?"

"That whooshing sound?" Elaine stands from her bed, stretches. Color floods back to her cheeks. Fresh crops of hair sprout from the thinned patches on her scalp, and the light returns to her eyes. She touches the top of her head and examines her hands with her mouth open wide.

"Well, that was pretty fucking weird."

"It worked!" I rush to her side and wrap her in a hug.

She hugs me back, and a lightning bolt of pain sears through my chest, followed by a loud CRACK. I can't breathe.

"Oh my god!" Elaine said. "Are you okay?"

"No." I hold my side. "I think you broke my rib bone."

"Oh no," she said. "Does that mean…"

"I reversed whatever fucked up spell this is," I say, wheezing. "The only problem is, now it's back on me."

"We've gotta get you to a hospital then," Elaine says. "I'm feeling one hundred percent better. Let's go! Come on, I'll drive!"

"They can't help me," I say, wincing at the pain. "There's only one thing I can do to stop this now."

"What?"

"I need to kill the person who did this to me," I say. "And I think I know how."

Chapter Twenty-Three

Rotting away fucking sucks. I know now that I always took my health and youth for granted, and never imagined a day when my body would fail me. Well, certainly not a day so soon. Even though I never really abused my body with drugs or alcohol, I definitely didn't appreciate what I had. All the times my muscles and bones worked, and how I never appreciated them. All the times I had strong hair, nails, skin, and teeth. If I get myself out of this situation, I'm going to be grateful. For my body. For my life. For everything.

I can't lie in bed and rot this time. Once the sun sets, Lydia and her ghoulish gal pals are probably going to pay me a visit, and I need to be ready. Even as my energy slips away from me, as strands of brittle hair dust my shoulders and my fingernails peel away from the quick, I know I'm not done yet. I didn't think I had anything to live for after Leo left me high and dry, after my dreams were smashed, and life became too hard to keep going. It was dumb to think giving up was the answer, but in the rearview, it wasn't like I had a big support system or mental and financial stability. I know now that I must live for myself, even if things seem bleak. I have something new to live for now, too—revenge. And it's one helluva drug.

My decaying body wants to lie down and let the bed consume me, to let the inexpensive sheets I got from Bed, Bath & Beyond (not stolen, but paid for with a forty percent off coupon) soak up my juices and liquified flesh. But my mind, my mind is alive again with artistic inspiration and elaborate revenge plots. I don't know what Lydia and her clique of ghouls are all about, but one thing's for certain, and it's that for them, image is literally everything.

She stole my soul with a photo? Well, I'll take control of hers with an image of my own.

The blank canvas that I had purchased from the mall still sits in the corner of my bedroom, waiting for me. Waiting for just the right time, gleaning inspiration from the universe as though its cotton skin knew its true purpose all along. It calls to me now, ready to fulfill its destiny. There was a reason I had bought a fresh canvas on the night that Lydia assaulted me—I know it now. There was a reason why I hadn't started a new project on it, why it sits there, waiting for the perfect opportunity to bring my vision to life.

I am going to paint a portrait of Lydia. I will show her what she really looks like. And then, I am gonna destroy her.

"Hey, how are you doing?"

Elaine pops her head into my bedroom as I set up my easel. She's back to her old self, brand new. It's like she was never accidentally cursed by me in the first place, and for that, I'm glad and grateful. If she permanently lost a toe or an earlobe or something because of me, I would never forgive myself.

"I'm falling apart," I tell her. "But I have work to do."

"This is all really weird," Elaine says. "I don't know what to think of everything. It all feels kind of crazy."

"Yeah. I thought so too," I said. "But after last week, I'll believe just about anything."

"What are you going to do?" she asks.

"I think that the woman who assaulted me, who did this to me—to us, I think she's going to come after me. Probably tonight."

"So call the cops," Elaine said. "We can get help. You don't have to do this alone."

"I do, though," I say. "I can't really explain it, but whatever this woman has or is or does, she seems to have superpowers. Not just like, sucking the life and energy from people, but also flying and mind control."

"Come on…"

"It's true. I think that's how she's gotten away with this for so long," I say. "I witnessed it myself. Some police came here interrogating me, and I swear I was able to just talk myself out of it."

"Police? Came here? Why?"

"It's a long story," I say. "Anyway, I was able to use my influence to get them off my back. I'm sure she's been doing the same for a long time."

"So you think she'll just charm the police or whatever?" Elaine asks.

"Yeah. Something like that."

Elaine shifted on her feet. "What will you do if she shows up then?"

I nod to the empty canvas. "I'm going to paint her portrait. Give her a taste of her own medicine."

"I don't understand."

"I can't say I do either," I say. "I just know that destroying an image seems to break the spell. Remember how you were sick, and I tore up the last photo I had of you?"

"Yeah."

"And how, after I tore up the photo, you were miraculously healed?"

Elaine nods. "I did seem to get better out of nowhere right after that."

"Well, this woman has a photo of me," I say. "I'll force her to give it back to me, or something. I dunno. First, I'm going to paint a portrait of her. Let her see what it feels like to have someone else pull the strings."

"And what if this doesn't work?" Elaine asks.

"I'm done for either way," I sigh, pick off the nail on my pointer finger, and show it to her. "I'm falling apart again. But I won't go down without a fight."

"What do you want me to do?" Elaine asks. "Like, if they come here tonight?"

"You should go to Leticia's," I say. "It's not safe for you here."

"It's not safe for you either," she says. "I really don't know what to think."

"I'll be fine. I know how to handle myself. You're a good friend, Elaine. I'm sorry I was so shitty to you."

"I'm sorry, too." Elaine goes in for a hug.

I reach for her and then think better of it. "I probably smell pretty gross."

"I don't care."

My best friend wraps me in a hug, and even though I hear my sternum frizzle and crack and my skin burns and stretches as though it's going to peel away from the muscle, her hug is the best thing ever. Feel-good chemicals flood my veins as we embrace, and I think for a moment that maybe I have it in me to do this. Maybe I'll be able to reverse whatever this curse is and get things back to the way they should be.

She lets me go, and I wipe a blood tear from my cheek.

"Thanks. I needed that. I can't remember the last time someone touched me and didn't want anything in return."

"That's so fucking sad." Elaine laughs and wipes her own glassy eyes. "You really want me to leave?"

I nod. "Yeah. I got it from here."

"Fuck. Okay," she says. "It doesn't feel right, but if that's what you want, I'll go."

"Love you."

"Love you, too."

Elaine closes my bedroom door, and it's just me and my canvas. I'm still wearing the red cocktail dress from the night before, and I don't feel like changing into anything else. The bones in my fingers ache with arthritis as I set up my station and stare at the easel. It's been so long since I've picked up a brush that I wonder if I'll even remember how to paint. But, just like riding a bike, I set up my colors and get the paint thinner, and it all starts coming back to me.

I close my eyes in front of the canvas and try to visualize what Lydia looked like the first night I saw her—those snarling, bloodless lips. Wild, buggy eyes. Skin the color of cement, thin and dry over a network of blue veins. Yes. I know her hideous face and exactly how I want to portray her, not as the young, vivacious hostess her cunty coven knows her to be. But the real her. The ghoul beneath it all. That's what I will paint. That's what I will show her.

I begin by painting a likeness of the hood of my car, the portrait being composed from my point of view behind the wheel. From there, I add her gnarled, claw-like hands and her fur coat. The canvas soaks up the paint, a palette of bruise hues in gray, black, purple, and royal blue as her face, her horrid fucking face, is recreated before my eyes.

Time ticks away, and I am unmoved in front of my canvas as I work, inspired once again by the very horrors that I've lived through. Every movement is excruciating, but I keep going and keep painting because I know that soon it will be dusk, and soon she will come for me. I keep going because I'm afraid that if I stop, something else will fall off my body. Something else will begin to rot, and maybe this time it will be my fingers or my eyes, and I may never get to paint again.

I'm nearly finished with the portrait when I hear my phone ring. I haven't checked my phone all day; in fact, I'd almost forgotten about it. Funny how I used to live and die by my phone, assessing my worth based on who has called or texted me. I finish my portrait and let the call go to voicemail.

The paint is still very wet when the light outside my window is no longer suitable for painting. I realize I've been sitting in front of my easel for ten hours—the entire day. My nervous system screams in pain, but I've achieved what I set out to do. I stand on atrophied limbs, the joints in my knees and ankles creaking like rusted hinges as I reach for my phone. There's a new voicemail from a number I don't recognize. I press the voicemail icon and bring the phone to my ear.

"Hey, it's me," Leo said. "I'm calling from a burner, I'm pretty sure you blocked my number again. Listen, I don't remember much of what happened the other night. I was really drunk, but I know that I was not nice to you, and, well, I just wanted to apologize, I guess. I know how that must sound, and I don't blame you if you don't believe me. My time in the hospital really got me thinking about everything. I was wrong, the way that I left and the way that I treated you." Leo pauses, takes a breath, and continues.

"Anyway, I'm going back to New York in a couple of days, and I'm not going to reach out to you again. My parents are getting me into an outpatient rehab program up there. I think it's time. I need to focus on my family and my life there. Anyway, I just wanted you to know, I'm sorry. Take care."

I delete the message and flip the phone closed.

"Bye, Leo."

I smile, despite the pain radiating in my hips and spine. It wasn't the closure I wanted from Leo, but it's the closure I got. I feel like, no matter what happens now, we can both move on and leave the past where it belongs. It's funny—with George, Leo, Ted, any of the people who have come to me wanting me to be their plaything on the side, I always ended up getting hurt. But ultimately, even if they hurt me, I never wanted to hurt anyone else, especially the people who loved my clients and depended on them. But that's not how the world works. We all end up hurting each other in the end. Pain is part of being human. It can't be avoided. You have to feel it, then you have to grow and move past the things that cause you pain, or they can destroy you and everyone you love.

The street lights outside my apartment blink to life, and the hairs on the back of my neck go erect. Every cell in my body vibrates with a sensation of doom as the sky darkens. I'm overwhelmed with a flood of fight or flight chemicals, but I'm too slow to act on the burst of energy. My limbs can barely respond as I edge toward my bedroom door. I need to leave. I need to run. But before I can make my escape, my kitchen door kicks open, and a dark, hulking figure fills my entryway.

Chapter Twenty-Four

"Just *look* at what you've done to my little Clementine!"

Lydia bursts through my kitchen in a hurricane of rage, spittle flying from her purple lips. She waltzes into my apartment, uninvited and effervescent with her signature brand of bubbling, barely bottled rage. Like usual, she's dressed in a fur coat, wild eyes masked behind oversized designer sunglasses. From her complexion and thin, dry hair, it's apparent that she's still drained of energy. Even though I was half-expecting my nemesis to show up at my door, I never could have anticipated the entrance she was making. Lydia didn't come alone; draped over her left shoulder is the strangest, saddest body I've ever seen.

"All you had to do was eat a single strand of hair. Was that so hard?" She brushes past me into my living room and utters a scoff of disgust. "Ugh. This little apartment is even more terrible than I imagined."

My mouth hangs open as she places the body on my living

room couch. In the low light, I can see that it's the size of a small child, dressed in a black lace gown and covered in tufts of gray and copper hair. I flip on the living room overhead light and gasp.

"What the fuck did you just put on my couch?"

The creature stares at me with violet eyes from beneath a mane of silken tan hair. Its face is a blend of human and canine features, with perfect, child-like ears and an elongated snout, black lips, and razor teeth. Its humanoid legs are hinged backwards at the knee like those of a jackal, and its fingernails are black claws. A long, furry tail wags weakly beneath the black lace skirt. The creature makes soft pants in short, sharp breaths and lets out a low moan.

"Can't you see that my daughter is in pain?" Lydia cries. "Don't you feel bad for what you've done?"

"What I've done?" I say. "Wait, is that…"

"Clementine, yes. God, get up to speed," she says. "I had to bring her here to show you. This is what happens when you break the circle. All you have to do is perform the transfer of energy, and the ritual will be complete."

"That's your dog?" Tears spring to my eyes as I remember the little Yorkie. I feel even worse now for ever thinking badly about the creature. "What did you do to her?"

"Not my dog, my *daughter*," Lydia says. "Well, she was supposed to transform into my daughter but you screwed everything up. Now look at her! Why did I ever think that you were ready for all of this?"

"I don't know, Lydia. I'm kind of a fuck up. That's on you." I can't stop looking at the pathetic little half-dog, half-girl. She looks so sad.

"First, you ruin my ceremony, and then you break the window in my vestibule. Do you know how expensive it is to replace that? I won't even be able to live in my home until the damage is fixed; the condo association won't allow it. You really have no sense of decency, do you?"

"Sorry. I didn't want to wait for the elevator."

Lydia sighs. "Look, you're tired; I'm tired. Everyone else in the group already did their energy exchange. You're the only one holding up the process. Just do the energy transfer and we'll all feel better."

"What will happen to—" I pause. "*Clementine,* if I do it?"

"She'll transform into my beautiful little daughter forever." Lydia sits on the edge of the couch and strokes the creature's hair.

"Why?" I say, overcome with emotion. Looking at the poor, pathetic little creature makes me sadder and angrier than anything I've witnessed yet. Of all of the cruel things that Lydia has done, this seems like, by far, the most bizarre and horrid. "Why would you do this?"

"Eternity is very lonely," Lydia says. "Of course, in my preserved state, I couldn't naturally have a child of my own. So I decided to make one."

"What about your friends?" I ask. "You made them, didn't you?"

"It's not the same." Lydia plucks a hair from the creature's head. "Enough talking. You need to eat this now. As soon as you do, Clementine will be free of pain. The circle will be complete, and our energies will be restored. Here. Take it."

Lydia shoves the strand of hair (fur?) into my hand. I don't know what to make of this situation, and any possible scenario

I conjured of our eventual showdown didn't lead up to this. I'm simply not prepared to make this decision. I don't want the little girl-dog thing to suffer, but I don't want this cycle to continue either.

"What will happen if I don't consume her…hair?"

"You'll consume it, one way or the other. The others will come to make sure of it," Lydia says. "They're not as nice as I am, unfortunately."

"I believe you," I say. "But, I don't want to live like this anymore."

"It doesn't matter. You're already mine," she says. "I need you to do this willingly, or it won't work."

"Give me back my photo and I'll do it," I say. "Let me have control of my image again."

"No deal," Lydia says. "Unless you want to trade for someone else's energy. Where is that girl who lives with you anyway?"

"Stay away from Elaine," I say.

"Finish the ritual."

I take a deep breath and gaze at the poor, suffering creature again. Lydia is a fucking monster. I never hated anyone or anything with my whole body before, like I hate this woman. I would never heel to her, never comply. Even if I destroy myself in the process, maybe I can still spare the thing writhing on my couch. Maybe I can stop Lydia and keep Elaine safe. I have to think quickly. I have to try *something*.

"Okay, okay. I'll do it," I say. "I just need to get a drink from my room to wash it down."

"Good," Lydia says. "Hurry up. This transformation process is very painful for Clementine."

I wince and take one last look at the girl dog. What if Lydia is lying about Clementine, too? What if that's just some random little girl she snatched off the street and experimented with? I may never know.

I drag my weak and weary carcass to my bedroom, drop the strand of hair to the floor, and pick up the canvas. I can only hope that painting the portrait of Lydia has worked. She's weaker than yesterday, so I have hope that maybe the magic of the portrait has already begun to work. This painting is my only bargaining chip. An image for an image. A life for a life. She gives me back my Polaroid, and I give her the portrait.

"Hurry up in there!" Lydia calls out. "The circle is only open for twenty-four hours. We'll have to wait a whole other year to perform the ritual if you don't do it now."

My body feels sluggish, my pulse barely rising as I grip the side of the portrait and walk back toward the living room. Lydia is hunched over the creature, her features pinched and full of something close to worry or concern, though I can't imagine that her shriveled heart truly cares for anything else. She pets the creature's head and is cooing softly at it when I step into the living room with her portrait in my hand.

"I made you something," I say. "It's been a while since I completed a project, but I think it turned out okay. What do you think?"

Lydia removes her sunglasses and gazes at me. Her purple irises go black as she stares at her own horrid likeness. The corner of her thin lips twitches, and her pinched expression falls.

"What is that?"

"This is a portrait I painted of you," I say. "It's from the first night we met. I think it's a pretty good likeness."

"Give it to me," her voice trembles.

"No."

"I'll end you," she snarls. "Then I'll find your fuckass roommate and devour her soul. I'll find your sad, lonely mother and stomp out her cats one by one. I'll find your alcoholic boyfriend and eat his baby alive while he watches. I'll kill everything you've ever loved."

My body tenses as she continues her tirade. I don't doubt for a moment that she would do any of the things that she threatened me with. Still, I stand my ground.

"All I'm asking is for a trade," I say. "Your image for mine."

"I'll tear off your skin and feed it to Clementine before that ever happens."

"Don't threaten me with a good time."

"Give it to me!" Her voice gurgles. Her mouth is full of blood.

"No."

"Okay then." She hocks a glob of red mucus on the floor. "Have it your way."

Lydia sails through the air across my living room with her arms outstretched and clawed hands flexed. Her hands close around my throat as she crashes into the painting and pushes me backward. My head slams into the wall, and a frisson of skull fractures fills my ears like the crinkling of Christmas wrapping paper. Her fingers tighten around my neck, and starbursts float in front of my vision as the world goes black.

Chapter Twenty-Five

Well, fuck.

Why did I think that my plan to stop Lydia would work? Why did I think that I would ever be anything but a big old failure? At least now I'm dead, and I don't have to worry about slowly falling apart anymore. It would have sucked to witness losing my toes and fingers and ears and nose, to lie helpless as my skin gets sticky and tacky like old Barbie doll legs. At least now I can rest.

Except, I can't rest. The back of my head feels like a watermelon dropped on hot pavement, my brains a slop of mushy pink flesh speckled with black seeds. A stabbing sensation rips through my ribcage like when I had to run the mile in sixth grade, only worse. A new stitch works its way into my side every time I inhale, knifing me over and over again. Goddammit, I'm still breathing. That bitch hasn't killed me yet. This piercing, throbbing headache makes me wish that she did, though.

"Babe? Babe, are you okay?"

Elaine's voice is all echoey, like she's talking to me underwater through an empty hallway. I try to tell her no, to tell her to get away, but I can't get my mouth to work. A thin sliver of light pushes through as I coax my eyelids to open. I'm on the floor. I'm in pain. And Lydia is moving on top of me.

"You stupid, useless…" Lydia moans, shaking her head side to side. The portrait is sandwiched between our bodies, somehow still intact. I tilt my body to the side, hold on to the painting, and roll her off of me.

"Are you okay?" Elaine's hands are under my armpits. She pulls me to my feet, and I stare down at my attacker. "What the hell is that thing on our couch?"

"It's Clementine," I say. "Elaine, you shouldn't be here."

"Oh my god. What is that? Some kind of Halloween decoration?"

"No. She's a Yorkshire terrier that bitch tried to turn into a real girl." I deliver a kick to Lydia's gut. She groans and curls into a ball. "That's some sick ass Pinocchio shit!"

"You were right. You were right all along." Elaine shakes her head, her eyes bugged wide. "What should we do?"

"My plan didn't work. She won't give me my photo back," I say. "I don't know what to do."

"Destroy her painting," Elaine says. "That has to work, right?"

"Fuck, you're probably right," I wince. Being alive hurts too much. "It's worth a try."

"Noooo," Lydia moans.

She's on her feet before I have time to fully recover. She

reaches for me, *Night of the Living Dead* style, as I hold tight to her portrait like a shield. She'll have to pry the canvas from my severed hands.

"Elaine! Get me a knife!" Red spittle sprays from my lips. I really took some damage in that collision. I think I might not make it this time.

"Here!" Elaine is two steps ahead of me. I extend my hand, and she places a serrated knife in the center of my palm. "A steak knife?"

"The other kitchen knives aren't clean!"

Lydia stumbles toward me, woozy and off-kilter. Her left hand looks melted, and half of her hair is gone. Her jaw sits funny in her skull, like it's been knocked out of alignment. She must have taken some damage in the collision, too.

"This will have to do," I say. " Goodbye, Lydia."

I hold out the canvas, bring my hand back, and stab through the painted fabric. One slice. Two slices. Three. Lydia's horrific portrait is slashed down the middle, her face segmented like an unholy triptych. I try to raise my arm to go for a fourth slash, but I'm losing energy. I'm damaged and weak, and even though my opponent is losing steam too, I still need to finish this. I go to stab her painting again when she warbles toward me.

"You bitch, look what you've done to me."

Lydia is no longer intact. Well, from the waist up anyway. Like her sliced portrait, her head and torso are in pieces, split three ways down the middle like a flayed hot dog. There's surprisingly little blood considering the severity of her wounds, but then, her insides are mostly mummified organs and dust.

"It still didn't work!" I say, slashing at the painting again.

"Wait, look at her hand!" Elaine says. "On the painting. Where the paint was still wet, look!"

Elaine is right. Lydia's body must have smudged the painting during our fight. The same hand melting off on Lydia's actual body is the hand I painted.

"Go get my turpentine!" I say.

"Got it!"

Elaine disappears into my bedroom as Lydia grips the canvas with her remaining good hand.

"I should have destroyed you…" the three-headed Lydia creature garbles. "You didn't deserve this gift. Stupid, lazy girl. Wasting your precious life."

"Waste this."

With my last bit of energy, I curl my right hand into a fist, pull back my arm, and punch Lydia in her hideous, crooked mouth. My fist connects with her pearly little teeth as I feel a pop in my arm socket. The flesh on my upper arm rips away, and the bone disconnects from the shoulder like a hot wing. Something falls to the floor with a thud.

My right arm. My dominant hand. *Fuck!*

Lydia falls backward, and the painting crashes to the ground. Elaine returns to the living room with the paint thinner, her wild gaze jumping from my severed arm to the painting to Lydia's monstrous form writhing on the ground. Clementine pants but remains motionless on the couch, a witness to it all.

"Douse the painting, Elaine!" I say. "Now!"

Elaine unscrews the top of the can and pours out the rest of the contents of the turpentine onto the canvas. The effect is almost immediate. Lydia screams, and her skin bubbles, but she's not melting fast enough. She's on her feet again, clawing at her segmented torso with her remaining hand.

"We need to rub it in!" I shout to Elaine. "Get a washcloth!"

Lydia and I scramble to the canvas at the same time. I forget that I'm missing an arm and try to pick it up with both hands, but only manage to grab one side. Lydia's goopy hand closes in on the other side of the shredded, tacky paint portrait. She tries to tug the painting away from me, but I hold fast.

"You can't destroy me." Lydia laughs, and a spray of red slaps my cheek. "I am *eternal*."

Elaine comes up behind Lydia with a dish towel in her hand. We make eye contact and nod.

"You're toast."

Elaine brings her knee to her chest and delivers a front kick to Lydia's torso. Her foot connects with what's left of her back, and the kick sends her soaring. Her monstrous form crashes into my coffee table, the collision causing a segment of her split upper body to fall away. Elaine holds the canvas upright as I use my left hand to wipe away the turpentine-soaked oil paint.

"You bitch, you absolute cu—" Lydia garbles, reaching for me.

I wipe her outstretched hand on the canvas, furiously scrubbing the image. Lydia's arm melts away as I erase, but I don't stop there. I wipe away her shredded face and let out a cackle as her lips recede and liquify. I turn the portrait I worked so hard on into a swirl of gray, circling and rubbing, blotting out her hideous image. Just like George, her eyes bulge and pop like grapes, her insides bursting and puddling down her frame, exposing an ivory skeleton. I rub and rub, eliminating the image of her I created until there's nothing left of my attacker but a puddle of pink goo and an expensive fur coat.

Chapter Twenty-Six

In March, Elaine moved in with Leticia, and Clementine and I moved back in with my mother. We didn't get our deposit back on the apartment because the stain Lydia's body left on the living room floor wouldn't come out. Elaine was understanding about it all. I miss living with her.

Clementine is a good little dog. I feel like shit for ever thinking badly about her. She was only ever doing her job and protecting her mistress, and what a fucked up mistress she was. Thankfully, after Lydia's body was fully liquified and gone for good, whatever weird ass ritual she was trying to perform on Clementine reversed. She seems to be no worse for wear. The vet says she's a healthy dog, in great shape, and probably around two years old. She gave my mom's Persian cats a hard time at first when we moved in, but they all get along now.

I'm still missing my right arm. Like my pinky toe, after Lydia was liquified and I regained my energy, the appendage didn't grow back. Thankfully, everything else has returned to its former state: my skin, hair, and nails, all of it. I still get headaches sometimes, though, probably from when Lydia rammed me into the ground. My skull may never fully recover from our tussle, but at least my head didn't crack open in the fall and spill my brains to the ground.

To tell the truth, my mother was more upset than I was about me losing my arm. I didn't know how to tell her how it happened. There wasn't exactly an easy way to explain it, and telling the truth wouldn't help either. Elaine and I decided to concoct a reasonable-sounding scenario—we were riding bikes at night, and a car sideswiped me. Like my toe, the area is closed up now, smooth and healed over as though the damage never even happened. I can still feel my phantom limb from time to time, a hand that reaches out to grasp a paintbrush or to stroke Clementine's silky head. A hand that isn't there. I gave my pinky toe and arm a burial at sea. The creatures of the gulf can have the long-lost parts of me. I like the idea that pieces of me remain out there in the ocean, consumed by some shark or fish or sea turtle.

I'm learning how to paint with my left hand now. It's frustrating, but I'm getting my technique down. My style has changed too, including my color palette, which isn't as soft and sweet as it used to be. I favor darker colors now, black backgrounds with only splashes of color here and there for dramatic effect. I painted another portrait of Lydia, just in case the first one didn't work all the way. The new composition doesn't look as good as the first one I painted, but it holds the same meaning. I keep it tucked away in the back of my closet, facing the wall.

Classes start for me at Remington in the fall. I hope they'll let me bring Clementine along as my emotional support companion. She goes everywhere with me now, growling at strangers and always standing guard. I love her so fucking much.

I'm also done with the sugar baby life, and with my foot model business, too. I'm pivoting to better support this new era of self-discovery. There's this new thing called YouTube where you can upload videos, and I've started documenting my progress as an artist who is learning to paint again after a traumatic injury. I also started an online business selling my artwork on coffee cups, t-shirts, mouse pads, that kinda thing. People love my Clementine portraits.

Even though I wasn't cut out to be a sugar baby, I have all the respect in the world for those who can hang in there with it. This life is tough, and there's always someone out there who wants a piece of you. We all need to do what we have to in order to survive. Clementine survived her painful transformation, and I'm going to survive, too. Life is hard, but I'm harder. Even though I had to lose a toe and an arm to figure it out, I'll never take this life for granted again. I'll never let someone control me or make me question myself again.

Thanks to Lydia's melted corpse, I'll never have to worry about anything ever again.

Epilogue

20 YEARS LATER

"Elaine! Leticia! You made it!"

I pass Clementine to my agent, Shelby, and embrace my old friend and roommate in a one-armed hug. It's been a long time since we last saw each other in person, but Elaine looks exactly the same as I remembered, only now with stylish streaks of silver through her close-cropped hair. Leticia looks much the same, though curvier and softer since becoming a mother.

"Did you bring the boys?"

"No, we left them back in Florida," Leticia says, pecking me on the cheek. "We haven't had a chance to get away since the twins were born. This is kind of a nice getaway for us."

"Oh, I was looking forward to meeting them!" I frown. "I'm going to have to try to make it back home to visit. I haven't been back since the funeral."

"I know, we were sorry to hear about your mother." Elaine frowns. "She would be so proud of you tonight."

"She would," I say, gazing up at her portrait. The image of my mother smiles down at me from the gallery wall at Space, SoHo. She's part of my latest collection, *Future Ghosts*. The *New York Times* art critic called my series of portraits haunting and playful, yet self-assured.

"I was so surprised to hear you would be showing your work here," Leticia says. "This isn't a very well-known gallery."

"I was surprised too," Shelby says, raising her eyebrows. Shelby is young and hungry, just getting her start in the art world. Sometimes my agent gets too many stars in her eyes. I know she's worried about commissions and sales, but I'm not. My gallery showings and auctions always sell out. Every. Single. Time.

"That's why I selected this place," I say. I motion for my dog, and Shelby returns Clementine to me. The little creature cuddles into the crook of my arm, forming her furry body to my side. "There are a lot of talented, unknown artists who show their work here. I wanted to try to highlight their work alongside mine."

"That's so generous of you," Leticia says. "Well, we are going to take a spin around the gallery."

"Perfect. Are you both staying nearby? We should get breakfast in the morning."

"We would love that," Elaine says. Her gaze darts to my missing arm, and she gives me a sad half-smile. She's kept our secret for two decades now, never telling a soul about that terrible night in our apartment. Sometimes I wonder if she's told her wife about what happened with me and Lydia, though Leticia has never given me reason to believe she knows. If I had a romantic partner, I would likely tell them a secret that big. Fortunately, I only have time and patience in my life for my art and Clementine.

Dozens and dozens of visitors and patrons stream in and out of the gallery all night, sipping on champagne and feasting on the canapes that are included with their door ticket. A number of pretentious art star types and even a few celebrities come up to me to gush about my work, in particular *Girl with a Flip Phone* (2009), a self-portrait I styled in the spirit of Vermeer's famous painting of a similar name. I'm kind and grateful to everyone who wants my attention, but keep our interactions surface-level and make sure to redirect their attention to some of my favorite student pieces housed in the gallery. I don't let many people get close to me these days, but I still have to surface into society now and then to sell my wares. Might as well try to do some good for others while I'm at it.

As the evening winds down, a familiar face comes into view, though one weathered with hardships and time. Leo has much less hair these days, though I would recognize him anywhere. At his side is a girl of about twenty with his eyes and smile. She breaks off to look closer at my portrait of Clementine in her half-dog, half-girl state (*Girl Dog, Interrupted* 2026), and he approaches me, trying to affect a boyish charm. Clementine senses my distaste and growls.

"Hi."

"Leo. What a nice surprise."

"I've been following your career for a while now. Wow."

He nods and pulls a half smile, hugging his arms to his chest. "Really impressive."

"Thanks." I motion to his companion. "Is that your daughter?"

"Yeah. She's a big fan of yours, too. An art student, like her old man." He laughs, scratches the bridge of his nose.

My gaze flicks to his ringless left hand. Either his marriage didn't work out, or it never happened in the first place. I never cared enough to discover.

"Well, thank you for stopping by," I say.

"Yeah, of course," he says. "I always felt bad for the way we left things, you know? And then I found out about your arm, and, ah, geeze. You were so sick back then, and all I could think about was myself."

"I know," I said. "It's okay. It's all in the past now."

"But, hey, you learned how to paint again!" He lets out a chuckle and hugs himself again. "You know, it isn't my style, but people really seem to like your work."

Clementine tenses in my arms. For a moment, I fantasize about letting her loose on Leo, allowing my companion to chew on his nose and lips so he'll shut up. But then I remember the young woman admiring my paintings and the promise I made to myself all those years ago. I purse my lips and fake a smile.

"I need to go find my agent," I say. "It was good to see you. If your daughter ever needs a recommendation, please tell her she can drop my name."

"Wait!" he says, his eyes wide with desperation. "I was hoping maybe, since you're in town...I dunno, I thought maybe we could have dinner or something."

My lips part, and I show him my teeth. "Not a fucking chance."

Clementine gives him one last warning bark for good measure as I turn and walk away.

Shelby is flirting with the handsome gallery owner, Marcus, as I make my final rounds for the evening. The event is winding down, and I'm getting tired, the fracture in the back of my skull hissing at me, signaling that I'm ready to call it a night. One last lingering group of women remains by the entrance, staring up at my latest portrait of Lydia. She's my favorite subject to paint. I can never seem to get her face to look perfect, though, but that's all part of the charm of her portraits. Something in her smile is never quite right, always crooked and smudged.

One of the women turns and glances at me as they exit the gallery. Her eyes flash lavender. She gives me a soft, knowing smile and a nod before disappearing into the night.

After all the patrons and guests left for the evening, Shelby has good news for me—all but one of my paintings sold. My next year of living as a working artist will be funded, though money is never an issue for me. I have a studio in Santa Fe. An apartment in Toulouse. My mother's house in Florida. So many places I call home, many investments, many bank accounts fat with a steady flow of funds.

"Let me call you a cab," Shelby says, linking arms with Marcus. He looks like a young Basquiat, only shorter. "You seem exhausted."

"I'll walk," I say. "I don't mind. Besides, Clementine could use the exercise."

"Okay, well, don't forget, we have that brunch with the docents at eleven," she says. "Get some rest."

"I'll be sure to come with an appetite," I smile. "And thank you, Marcus. You have quite an eye for talent. Your student pieces are tremendous."

"Thank you so much," he says. "You're welcome at Space any time."

"Goodnight."

I slip on my fur cape and sunglasses, and Clementine and I are off for our nightly walk. I gave up wearing coats long ago; capes are easier to put on and much more useful for my purposes, and besides, they look more stylish. It's been a while since I'd visited the city, but I love the feel of the sidewalk beneath my feet and the energy in the air as we trot block by block. I take my time, waiting for just the right moment, but the opportunity doesn't present itself. Not a single person catcalls me, panhandles me, or tries to mug me. This city is simply not as dangerous as it used to be.

It's midnight, and I have better luck near a dive bar. Clementine is patient as we watch from the shadows, observing the patrons as they go in and out. We've chosen a sports bar this evening, known for hosting frat boy types, a rarity in this part of the city. After a few minutes, a big, blond specimen stumbles onto the sidewalk, sucking on an electronic smoking device like it's a pacifier. He sways on his feet, and we lock eyes. In that brief exchange, I scan his thoughts, learning everything I need to know about him with one look. Oh, he's a bad one. This is going to be good.

My pink flip phone still works, though I decommissioned it for day-to-day use long ago. It no longer has cell service, but is still a convenient little storage device for my images. My ugly beauties—people who look good on the outside but are irredeemable inside. I snap a photo of his face illuminated in the street light and slip the phone in my pocket.

"Come, Clementine," I say. "Time to go home."

We walk past the man, and I give him one last chance to be kind, to give me any kind of sign that he isn't worthy of what I'm about to do to him. He does not acknowledge me, only hocks a healthy glob of lung butter onto the pavement near my feet. I place Clementine's leash in my mouth and pluck a wheat colored hair from the top of his head as I pass him by. It makes a pleasant crunching sound between my molars as we disappear into an alley.

"Well, that was easy," I say to Clementine and scoop her under my arm. "I'm tired. Should we take the scenic route home?"

Clementine sticks out her tongue and pants with approval. A rush flows through my body, and I know that I have been rejuvenated again, for how long this time, I couldn't say. The boy's life force is thick and edgy and plumps up my cells, regenerating my skin better than any filler or hyaluronic serum on the market. My feet lift off the ground, and I hover, higher and higher until I can see over the top of the bar, over the top of the adjacent apartment buildings, to the soaring New York skyline beyond.

Acknowledgments

Bed Rot Baby is a book that's lived in my heart for a long time, and it wouldn't be possible without the love and support of so many.

Thank you to my husband and sons for always supporting my creative works. It means so much to have the time and space to create and be my authentic self.

Thank you to my parents, Laura and Kevin Owen, for nurturing my weird girl inclinations from a very young age.

Thank you to my best friend and former roommate Teri for struggling through the early '00s with me and beyond. I would give an arm and a toe for you.

Thank you Cassandra, Lisa, Alma, Kayla and everyone at Quill & Crow Publishing for your tireless work polishing my little pink horror tale.

Thank you Faye Lane as always for your beautiful cover design.

Thank you Grace and Damien for always allowing me to scream in your DMs. I'm lucky to have fellow author friends like you.

Thank you to the legion of book reviewers, podcasters, booksellers, bloggers, and librarians who have supported my work along the way. Indie publishing is where boundaries are pushed in today's literary world, and my voice wouldn't be heard without your support.

And most of all, thank you reader for being here and spending time with me and Baby. I hope you loved reading her as much as I loved bringing her to life.

About the Author

Wendy Dalrymple loves to explore the beauty in horrific things. When she's not writing femme-focused #pinkhorror, you can find her hiking with her family, painting (bad) wall art, and trying to grow as many pineapples as possible. Find her at wendydalrymple.com

Thank You for Reading

Thank you for reading *Bed Rot Baby*. We deeply appreciate our readers, and are grateful for everyone who takes the time to leave us a review. If you're interested, please visit our website to find review links. Your reviews help small presses and indie authors thrive, and we appreciate your support.

More Feminist Horror by Quill & Crow

Credenza, Wendy Dalrymple

The Bone Drenched Woods, L.V. Russell

Ending in Ashes, Rebecca Jones Howe